PRESSY DAYS

Nilanko Mallik

Published by Woven Words Publishers OPC Pvt. Ltd., 2017

ISBN-13: **978-9386518194**

ISBN-10: **9386518198**

Price: ₹ 200

Woven Words Publishers OPC Pvt. Ltd.,
Vill: Raipur, P.O: Raipur Paschimbar, Dist: Purba Midnapore, Pin: 721401, West Bengal, India.
www.wovenwordspublishers.net

Printed by **Bhavish Graphics, Chennai**, India

WOVEN WORDS PUBLISHERS *Presents*

PRESSY DAYS

Nilanko Mallik studied at Presidency College, Kolkata (now Presidency University). He is a researcher in Neurolinguistics and Shakespeare in performance, and has been involved in writing of academic books and works of fiction. He heads a cultural unit, named *Shakespeare Youth Performances*, which is part of MIT's international project *Global Shakespeares*.

Besides academics, Nilanko Mallik is deeply interested in music, and plays the piano.

Website: https://nilankomallik.academia.edu

E-mail: nilankomallik@nlsr.org

CONTENTS

This book is dedicated

to

my undergraduate batch mates

ABOUT THE BOOK

Pressy Days is a collection of short stories and plays – which are based on the eventful life at Presidency College, Kolkata (now Presidency University). The book seeks to commemorate the days of English Hons. and the fun-filled life we had in the undergraduate days. All stories and characters are fictitious, but there are occasional glimpses of real incidents, which are told in the footnotes.

These footnotes are an attempt to reverse their purpose – footnotes are associated with academic books. Here, they have been given for a purely non-academic purpose, to add humour, and to make the stories liven up with life.

The title of the book is inspired by R.K. Narayan's *Malgudi Days*. Malgudi is fictitious. Presi is real. There is also a pun on the title. Presidency is haunted by reporters who flock for news, and so, there is a pun on "press" in the title. Furthermore, every student will admit the tremendous volume of studies which all Presidencians have had to undertake, and the days were hard-"press"ed in that way also.

Despite the academic pressure, despite the pressing presses, our years remain golden, unfading in its beauty, adding more to the value as it gets older. It is my expectation that the book will be well-received.

Nilanko Mallik
Kolkata

2017

Location Information

I do not prefer the tedious task of reading through detailed descriptions of scenes – they ruin the flow of the play, so I feel. That is why I have given the information of certain scenes before the play. It would be well if the reader goes through this before reading the plays, and not keep this till the scenes come. Scene descriptions inside the play occur only if there is any special arrangement.

Outside College Gate

The gate is on the right-hand side of the audience – at the corner. It forms the right exit. There should be book stalls at the back of the right stage and central stage, after which the road begins. The gate is collapsible.

College Gate

This scene is, as the name suggests, at the College Gate, but not as seen from outside. The view is from inside the college. So, the gate is at the left corner of the stage. A room – one of the staff quarters and used by the gatekeepers – stands at the back of the left stage. Trees outline the rest of back stage.

College Campus

This is actually the path leading to the main building of the college from the college gate. As such, it is a continuation of the previous scene. Trees stand at the back of left stage. There is a statue of Derozio at the back of centre-stage, followed by trees once again. There are two pillars at the two corners of right stage, marking the beginning of the main building. These two pillars form the right entry/exit.

College Portico

There are two pillars at right corners, and two pillars at left corners. The pillars at the left corner are the back side of the pillars found in College Campus scene. The four pillars form the porch. The pillars at left form the left entry-exit; the ones on the right form the right entry/exit. There is a cemented bench carved out of the wall of the porch, and is at the back of the centre stage. The rest of the stage is walled.

College Corridor

The pillars of the corridor stretch from the centre of left stage to the centre of right stage. The back stage is outlined by trees, with the statue of Derozio at the centre of back stage. The pillars are joined by railings.

Room No. 23

The door to this historic room is the left entry/exit of the stage. The Professor's chair is at right corner, centre. Benches cover the space from left to right. There is a door at the back of left stage, marked 'Seminar Library'. Several almirahs are lined at several places of left stage, marked 'Honours Library Books'. The back stage is obviously walled.

Computer Room of the English Department

This room is at the side of the Room No. 23. The entry/exit is from left. Several computers are at right stage and centre stage. The chairs are twice the number of computers. There is also a television set with a DVD player at the back of left stage. There are several DVDs. The back stage is obviously walled.

The Lounge

The entry/exit is from right. The front stage is used for this scene. There are sofas to the left, centre and right stage. A switch-board is at the corner of right stage. There are two doors to the right – one for general entry/exit, as earlier specified; the other leading to a classroom. This door is shut. The Professors use this door to come out of the class, as is shown in one play.

The Arts Library

There are doors at right and left stage. The door at the left stage leads to the Reading Room. There are many racks to keep bags at the back of right stage. After that, at the back of centre stage, are many drawers. At the back of left stage, another set of drawers is placed. The drawers have labels on them. These make up the manual catalogue of books, filed chronologically through centuries. A computer is kept at the back of left stage, after the second set of drawers, where students can check the books instead of going through the chest of drawers.

The Arts Library – Reading Room

The entry/exit is from right. Several desks and chairs are placed at the front stage and centre stage, stretching from left to right. The back stage is filled with shelves of books.

The Staff Room (in general)

Exit/Entry is from left as well as right. Several tables are lined from left to right. All tables have drawers.

The Staff Room – Round Table

A round table, set with a glass top, is kept at centre stage, up front. Exit/Entry is from left as well as right. Chairs are kept as necessary.

SHORT STORIES

BOYS' DAYS OUT[1]

I

"Hi, I've some news for you!"

I looked up from reading The Oxford Dictionary and beheld Ankit and Harsh bending over me. It was Harsh who had spoken.

"Lower your voice," I said. "This is a library."

Harsh lowered his voice and spoke again.

"I've got this beautiful plan," he began. I wondered what it was this time, and looked over my oval glasses with a penetrating look in Harsh's eyes. In the meantime, Ankit sat down on the chair opposite me. Harsh took the chair beside Ankit.

"As I was saying," he continued.

"Are you two in this together?" I asked.

"Yes," said Ankit. "And Indra too."

I turned my eyes to penetrate Ankit's eyes.

"He's more muddled than Harsh," I thought, and looked at Harsh once more. "He's planning to go out – just the four of us," I thought.

"I think we can go camping during this puja vacation," said Harsh. "Just the four of us."

I gave a knowing smile. My God-gifted powers were always reliable.

"So, what do you think?"

"And all three of you have agreed upon this?" I asked.

"Yes," said Harsh, after a slight pause.

I looked at Ankit.

"Let's go," said Ankit. "It will be very lovely."

---

[1] The inspiration for this title is obviously the film title, *Baby's Day Out*.

15

"It will," I said, "but not for the four of us together. Do you seriously see the four of us doing anything together?"[2]

"This is our chance to do things together and prove we can do things together," said Harsh.

"If we were to do things together, we would have done them by now."

"Oh, Indra said the same thing at first," said Harsh. "You two should be together."

"We know we should not be – and cannot be – so we said so."

"Oh, come on, let's go," persisted Ankit.

"I have my students…"

"We'll go during the puja days. Surely your students will not come then?" asked Harsh.

"No, they won't," I said. "So, have you fixed the place of camping?"

"No, we will do that after we have all decided to go," said Harsh.

"I know some woods in Narendrapur where we can camp," I said.[3]

"SO YOU ARE GOING!" shouted Ankit.

"Quiet!" I hissed. "I must say I have always loved camping."

"Now we have to arrange for the tents," said Harsh.

"Well, I said, "one of my uncles is the ex-Director of the Geological Survey of India.[4] He will be able to provide us with two tents."

"That is splendid," said Ankit.

"So, you guys want to camp out in the woods of Narendrapur?"

"OF COURSE!"

"But we have to draw out a proposal," I said.

"For what?" asked Harsh.

"Exactly! For what?" asked Ankit.[5] He added, "And of what?"

---

[2] As a matter of fact, it was true. The four of us were like four corners of the earth. But we were friends in pairs.

[3] This might sound absurd (even to residents of Narendrapur), but there is actually a wood there. Not many people are aware of it. I found it out quite by accident while with one of my friends in my school days. Now, much of it is gone with so many houses being built, but there are some areas of it still left.

[4] This is actually so.

"Well, there are various aspects which we cannot stand about each other.[6] We will have to tolerate some of them – but there are still some aspects which we will never be able to tolerate. So, we have to agree that we will have to put those aspects beside ourselves when we are camping – or travelling – so that things can work out among us," I said.

I hoped they would not agree to it.

But they did. Harsh and Ankit both thought for some moments.

"You are right," said Harsh. "I'll go and fetch Indra."

He rose up and went outside the library. I looked at him till he had disappeared, and then turned towards Ankit, who was looking at the portraits of some professors and famous students of the college.[7]

"I was under the impression that you did not wish to have anything to do with Harsh," I said.

"I am under the same impression."

"Then why do you want to go out with him? You now quite well none of us will get along with each other!"

"That is exactly why I want to go."

"I don't think you understood me. You and I can get along to some extent, Dibya and Harsh can get along to quite some extent – but the four of us can't get together."

"I understand that perfectly. That is why I want to go. I want to show the world that we do not get along."

I looked at him pitifully. Before he could say anything more, Harsh re-entered the library, with Indra beside him. The two boys came up (Harsh enthusiastically and Indra majestically) and Harsh took his seat, while Indra looked around for a chair that would fit him,

---

[5] Ankit actually has the habit of saying things like this, after someone has already brought it to attention.

[6] This is the basic reason why we were like four corners of the earth while doing our undergraduate days.

[7] These portraits are actually there in the college Arts Library and the Professors' Common Room.

on which he could sit without breaking it. Finding none, he said, "I've been sitting all this while. I prefer standing."

Harsh took out a paper and pen and wrote 'List of Things We Must Not Do While camping or Travelling'.

Then, he looked up at the others.

"Divide it in four sections and write the names of each of us," I said. Harsh did it with patient perfection.

"Let us begin with me," said Harsh, in an obvious attempt to sound modest.[8]

"First of all, you must not smoke," I said.

"Exactly! You must not smoke," seconded Ankit.

"That's crazy," said Harsh. "You know I can't do that."

"Well, then, consider the trip cancelled."

"All right," sighed Harsh. "I will not smoke. There. I've written it." So, the list began. It took us quite some time, and another sheet was brought out.

"You must not keep nagging about rhetoric, prosody and grammar in general," said Harsh. I agreed after some deliberate protests.

"You must speak comprehensively," I said to Harsh. He grumbled.

So, the list went on and on. After about half-an-hour, we quit.

The list, so made, ran as follows.

Harsh

Must not smoke or drink

Must speak comprehensively

Must not lecture endlessly

Must abstain from the use of slangs

Must not talk about studies, courses and universities

Should talk least of girlfriend

Must not talk of politics

Saheb

Must not nag about rhetoric, prosody and grammar in general

Must not keep talking of students

Must eat as fast as possible

Must not confuse names

Should give least amount of penetrating looks

Must clean spectacles everyday

---

[8] This is an irony.

Ankit
Must not talk on and on – unless to make others fall asleep at night.
Must not be particular about speaking in Victorian English
Must not suggest being in the dark (literally)
Must not talk of politics
Should show least amount of lethargy
Must not talk of bi-polar disorder[9]
Must stop speaking to himself

Indra
Must not smoke or drink
Must not sing – unless to scare off wild animals
Must not brag
Must be able to lift himself up when needed
Should eat as less as possible
Must not take up must space in bed
Must not lecture
Must not talk about politics

After making the list, it came to our notice that there were several points which we were 'to do'. So, the heading was changed. The modified heading ran:

Codes of Conduct while Camping or Travelling.

We put our signatures at the end of the list, after which Harsh went to make three copies. Ankit accompanied him to see that nothing more was added or cut off; Indra went back to his place in the corridor.

II

It was a fine Monday morning. The sound of play-pistols was heard anywhere and everywhere. The pujas had begun. We four boys started out from our various houses in various parts of South

---

[9] After being admitted to college, he informed us of this suspicion.

Kolkata, not for pandal-hopping, but camping. This might sound unusual, but it did not matter to us when families and friends raised eyebrows, for our eyes were dancing higher than the reach of those eyebrows which were raised by convention.[10] For Faith is personal, and should be personally kept, and others should tolerate such personalities.

So it was that we four boys set out, each with a rucksack over his shoulder. We were all supposed to meet at Garia auto stand at 10:30a.m., from where we would take an auto to Sonarpur.

"I thought you said Narendrapur," Ankit had pointed out, when we were planning the journey.

"Yes," I said. "There are several ways in which one can reach Narendrapur. The place is really vague. It is at the left and right of Garia, then cut off by Sonarpur, and begins once more from its back side."

"Whatever," said Harsh. "It does not matter where it is as long as we know how to get to it."

So, it was decided that we would take an auto, drop down on the way to Sonarpur, and walk for some minutes to enter the woods.

"I have problems in walking," said Indra to Harsh.[11]

"None of us can carry you around, big guy," said Harsh.

"It's not far from where we get down," I said to Harsh.

Indra had remained silent to that, so it was taken to mean that he had given his assent.

Harsh and I were the first to arrive. Harsh had a cigarette in his hand.

"You are breaking the rules," I said.

"No, I'm not," said Harsh. "We have not yet reached camp."

I brought out the photocopied paper and read out.

"'Codes of Conduct while Camping *or Travelling*.' There. So, drop it."

"Oh, come on."

---

[10] These lines on religion, and the following lines on religion, are my views. No insult is meant to the festive occasion; I merely wish to point at the diversity of personal faith.

[11] Throughout the story, Indra and I do not speak to each other – Harsh is our means of communication.

"I am allergic to that smell."

"Then smell it and get used to it."

"You are going to drop it," I said in hard tone and looked at him over my glasses. This was a look which had always (except for once) served its purpose.[12] This was no exception. Harsh looked at the cigarette longingly, as if to take another puff, and then threw it out.

"You sound like a teacher," he remarked.

"I know."

We did not have to wait in silence for a long time, for Indra arrived within a few minutes. He began speaking to Harsh.

After fifteen minutes, I rang up Ankit. He said he was just coming out of his house, and would be there within ten minutes. After fifteen minutes, I called him up again.

"I am just getting out of my house," said Ankit.[13]

"Have you shifted your house to the bhulbhulaiya in Jaipur?" I asked.

"Of course not," came the irritated reply. "Do not be silly. I am coming."

After twenty minutes more, Ankit arrived, his face a big smile, his forehead lined, and he walked with a graceful air about him which showed that apparently, his innocence was still not driven out by the fierce father of adult experience, for he walked as if he had all the time in the world, and was to tutor elephants how to walk.

---

[12] The exceptional case will obviously not be told, but at that time, I did not have my glasses.

[13] An incident must be told here. While in our third year, there was a departmental picnic. Well, actually, the picnic was just for our year (I did not go to it, for I have problems with long bus journeys). I was told that everyone was supposed to arrive at a given time. Ankit was the last to arrive. Long after the bus was supposed to have started, which it did not, thankfully for him, he messaged one of the rest, saying that he was on the train (or waiting for one) and would arrive shortly.

Harsh was so full of eagerness to welcome this unadulterated scene that he reached forward and brought him to us. In the rush, the beautiful curtain was torn, and out emerged the irritated bull.[14]

"Behave yourself. Don't you dare to manhandle me."

"What took you so long?"

"I was packing in the morning."

"Don't you have the sense to walk fast when you are late?"

"I am not late. Perhaps a little bit. About ten minutes. That is no reason for me to walk hurriedly and ruin the excitement of going out for camping."

"You are fifty-five minutes late!"

"No, I'm not. My watch, which I have never timed, tells me that it is 10:40a.m."

"You need to time your watch."

"No, it shows the right time."

"Our watches, which we all time regularly with the time of Metro Railway (which is very punctual)[15] tells us that your watch does not show the right time."

"Yes, it does. My watch is perfectly correct."

"Well, let's get the auto now that we have all arrived."[16]

This statement was received with much eagerness by everybody.

So, we all boarded an auto ("One rupee extra for pujas," the driver had said aloud) and reached the destined point from which we were to walk into the woods.

It took us quite some time to get out of the auto (for Indra and luggage). Finally, we – and our bags – were all safely out of the auto, and crossed the road and began walking.

"Ooff," panted Indra.

"Lovely," said Harsh.

---

[14] Ankit's sun-sign is Taurus, the Bull.

[15] This was written before the extension of the metro railway to Garia, after which all the regular passengers faced the harassment of a very-frequently-delayed metro service for several years. However, the watches were always reliable.

[16] This remark came from either Indra or myself. I let it lie on the reader, in accordance with Roland Barthes and all the other post-structuralists.

"Just a bit more," I said.

Ankit said nothing, but looked at the trees by the side of the road, and wondered (as he later told us) if we could climb one to get some coconuts.[17]

Soon we came to a little clearing in the line of trees and entered the woods. The trees were now all around us – their leaves covered the ground. We walked on for five minutes before we came to a little clearing in the woods.

"This is the spot," I said.

"Lovely," said Harsh.

"Ooff," said Indra and sat down heavily on the ground. A few leaves flipped up due to the sudden rush of wind so caused by his long-desired abrupt sitting.

"This is great," observed Ankit.

"We can sit here for hours and hours at leisure," remarked Harsh.

"Now let's get to work," I said.

The others looked at me – wordless.

"Well, we have to set up the tents, at which none of us have any experience, and then light the gas and cook. It's 12:10p.m. We must get to work," I explained.

"It's 11:25a.m.," said Ankit. He looked up from his watch and received three murderous looks, and decided to fall in with us.

With resigned looks, Harsh and Ankit began unloading their bags. I took out one tent. I had given the other to Ankit (he stays near my house).[18] He was biting his lips in his efforts to take out the tent without taking out the things, for he had placed his tent at the very bottom of things.

After watching him for some time, Harsh snatched up the bag, took out everything and then threw the bag at him, all the while in a desperate attempt not to use offensive words. Ankit contorted his

---

[17] Two years after I this story was written, Ankit did reveal a similar inclination for mangoes on a tree growing just outside our department.

[18] This is actually so.

face in seeing all his things so rashly handled, and it was with Indra's placing himself in their midst (and creating an impassable barrier) to take out the small gas cylinder that they were unable to hit each other.

I took out my illustrated notes on how to set up a tent, which I had copied with haste while my uncle was explaining it to me in a matter-of-fact voice, and began to go through them. I realised that what I had copied in hurry could not be deciphered. So, I made up the instructions where they could not be read.

"So," I began, "I will read out the instructions step by step and you guys work accordingly."

"No way," said Harsh.

"You have to help too," said Ankit.

So, it was decided by initiative and plebiscite that Indra would read out the instructions, while we would work at it.

I was the one who worked most, as I had to help in setting up the tents as well as rush to Indra every few minutes to read out what I had written, for he could not read it. I also had to make up instructions, as I said, and that involved brain-work.

"Harsh," he would call out, "I cannot make this out."

I would go to his rescue, while Ankit and Harsh would extend a hand and a leg to cover up for me.

"Harsh," I would tell him," I have written that we must now pull up the tents."

This is how we worked. First, we spread the tents wide open on the ground. There were six holes in each of the tents – four at each corner, and two at the front and back sides. Yes, the tents were old-fashioned. The modern tents have not much difficulty to be put up. But they come at a huge price, so we decided to use my uncle's old tents, for they came free, and the only price we had to pay was our panting efforts.

We next had to tie the ropes around each hole, and tie the other end around some wooden pegs. The next part was tricky. We had to dig these pieces of wood into the ground, and the measurement had to be such that the tents could be lifted up. At first, we obviously made a blunder and could not raise the tent an inch. So, we had to dig them up and dig them back again, a little shorter in distance.

It was on the fourth time that we could raise up one of the tents. It was 1:30p.m. We still had to work on the other. Indra rushed inside when the first tent was raised up, and put a pole (which he had made by savagely attacking a bamboo tree and breaking off two bamboo poles, of which he put the first in this tent) inside so that it remained raised. Then, we rushed like mad to attach the two wooden poles at the front and back sides before the tent could collapse. At 2:00p.m., one tent was up. We were too hungry to put up the other tent.

III

Indra, who had been eying the gas cylinder with much longing all this while, went and lit it up before anyone could even make anything ready.

Harsh took out a frying pan, opened a tin and took out four eggs, and broke the eggs and poured them on the frying pan to make omelettes. He had forgotten to pour a little oil in the frying pan.

"Ant," he called to Ankit. "Don't just stand there laughing at me. Go get the oil."

"It's inside your bag."

"Well, then take it out."

"I'm not as indecent as you are. I do not go through others' private properties."

I got up and brought the cooking oil, and another container. Harsh poured the eggs inside the container and with some leaves, began to clean the frying pan before pouring the oil.

"That is not hygienic," remarked Ankit.[19]

"We are camping in the woods, not eating in a five-star hotel," said Indra.

Ankit came and snatched up the frying pan.

"I'll wash it," he said.

"Where?" asked Harsh.

"Well, I'll go with him and see if we can find a pond," I said.

---

[19] Ankit is famous for his over-cleanliness.

So, we went together. After about five minutes, the ground became soft and wet, and in a minute, the sparkling water peered at us from the branches and leaves of the trees, and motioned us forward with a sly smile.[20]

Ankit took a handful of water from the pond, and poured it on the pan.

In fifteen minutes, we were back.

Harsh was ready to pour the oil.

"Wait," I said, rushing to my bag. "The water of the pond was not very clean. I mean, not clean enough."

I took out a bottle of mineral water, and washed the pan with it."[21]

"Now," I said, "we can pour the oil."

In his angry eagerness, Harsh poured too much oil, and had to put it back.

The eggs in the other container were all bonded together in a great tie of friendship in such a short while.[22]

We debated what to do.

"Let's make one giant omelette and share it among us," said Indra.

That was a good idea, but the frying pan was not good enough. Finally, it was decided to pour half of it in the pan at a time and make two semi-giant omelettes.

So, at about 3:35p.m., the omelettes were ready. Harsh handed out paper plates and we ate the omelettes, of which Indra obviously got the lion's share. Then, we opened our tinned food, and ate fried-rice. We were half-way through it when it struck us that Ankit was entrusted to bring tinned meat.

"I do not remember putting it inside," he began, at which he received cannibal-like looks from Harsh and Indra, and went to see if he *had* brought *it*.

"Why do you trust this fellow so much?" asked Harsh to me.[23]

---

[20] I must tell over here that when I first read this story to two of my friends, one of them asked, after I read this part, "This is understood, but why is the water behaving like a Hindi film heroine?"

[21] The reader must realise that it was extremely stupid of us to go to the pond in the first place, when this solution lay so near us.

[22] That is, all the eggs were mixed up.

[23] This is a question which Barnali had actually asked me.

"That is a matter between Ankit and me," I remarked.[24]

Ankit *had* brought it, and we ate till our stomachs were filled. The quantity of food was sufficiently lessened by then.

IV

It was 4:00p.m. when we finished eating. We all felt stinky, and it was decided that the pond, whose water was not fit for washing utensils, was good enough for us to bathe in.

"But is it really?" voiced Ankit.

"Shut up," said Harsh. "There is great fun in bathing in a pond while camping."

"But is it really?" voiced Ankit, again.

"So, what do you suggest?" asked Harsh.

Ankit thought hard for a few minutes.

"I suggest we get the water from there and boil it over here and purify it of germs, and then leave it to cool, and then bathe in warm free germ water."

"What?" spat Harsh.

"I mean warm germ-free water, or germ-free warm water," corrected Ankit.

"That is great," said Indra. "I am sure you do not mind sleeping in a wet tent."

"Aha," interjected Ankit, "try to understand. Who's talking of bathing inside the tent? We will do it in the cover of the bushes. We will arrange the tree leaves in such a manner so as to form a hidden spacious place."

This idea did appeal to all of us. However, opposition for the sake of opposing is one of the golden principles in which India functions in practical life. Harsh decided to oppose, undertaking the responsibility of seeing that the golden principle was not violated.

---

[24] This is an allusion to *Harry Potter and the Order of the Phoenix*, where Harry asks Dumbledore why he trusts Snape so much. Dumbledore replies that that is a matter between Professor Snape and himself.

"Pond is better," he said, and went with Indra to find the pond. They returned after half-an-hour, which was really surprising, for I'd thought they'd bathe for over half-an-hour in the pond, being so delighted.

"What happened?" I asked.

"Well, we did reach the pond, but just as we were about to strip and jump into it, Indra thought he saw something at the other end – inside the pond."

"It looked like an alligator," said Indra.

We decided to go with Ankit's idea. It was good too, for none of us were too eager to expose our natural selves in front of the others. Exposure in a football field, or after any other game is all right, but it is not at all a welcoming prospect in front of people with whom we do not get along well. This is characteristic of all civilized men; no matter the machoness or the physique. Models are exceptions, and I am sure there are not many models. The western world is ahead of us in this respect, for they are able to shed-off their fear with clothes.

We were all of us secretly thinking how to do our morning ablutions, but none dared to bring up the subject, till this moment.

"That's great, Ankit," I remarked. "We also need to make another such cover – to attend nature's call. My uncle told me we must dig up holes for this purpose."

The western world has solved this problem too, by coming up with make-shift toilets, easy to carry at the back of a car. But it costs much, and we came in autos and our feet, and preferred what we could do freely (there is a wordplay on this word)[25], the cost being only efforts.

We had each brought two mugs, but no buckets. A mugful of water would not do for bathing, and we couldn't do without bathing. So, I used my brain to come up with an invention then and there. I took some bamboo-leaves, threaded them up together, used my skills of origami to bring it to a proper shape, which would enable us to carry water in it.[26]

---

[25] The first meaning is free of cost. The second meaning is candidly. The second meaning is an irony.

[26] I have actually never done anything of this sort, though I do know origami.

Harsh was the first to try my invention. The process was very time consuming, but in the end, he emerged, fresh and gleaming, ready to sweat in the raising of the other tent.

It was 5:35p.m., before each of us had a bath, except me, for I do not bathe in such odd hours. Then, we got to working in raising the other tent. We had already tied up the ropes. All that remained was to put the wooden poles and raise up the tent. It was 7:00p.m. when the tent was finally raised up. We felt hungry and began to grope about in the dark for the tinned food. We had brought some cheap Chinese lamps, much better than the branded emergency lights, but did not think fit to light them up, for fear of wasting their charge.

So, we ate in the dark. After that, it was really dark, and we lit one lamp.

"Just look at the mess!" cried Ankit.

We were sitting in front of the tents.

"What mess?" said Harsh.

"All these tins and papers!" exclaimed Ankit.

"Don't worry," I said. "We will gather them up and dig some holes and put all these bio-degradable products inside them, and carry the tins back with us."

"They may be blown away!"

"The better for them and us," said Harsh gruffly.

That was a wrong thing to say, for Ankit poured a lecture for about half-an-hour on environment pollution. All of us got up to bring mosquito-repellent creams at this opportunity. When we came out, we saw Ankit was already picking up the papers and tins and putting them inside his bag, which he had (thankfully!) emptied of its contents.

Indra brought out his radio and began to listen to a popular (for the time-being) Bengali song of a band. I did not like it, as I do not like it, and began to play Celine Dion on my tape recorder.[27] Harsh put on earphones and listened to we do not know what, and Ankit, after finishing his exercise, turned on his radio to listen to political discussions.

---

[27] Sadly, this device is no longer to be found.

This was clearly against the rules, and I pointed that out.

"I'm not breaking any rule," he said.

Harsh and Indra took the opportunity to oppose their opponent.

"Yes, you are," said Harsh.

"You are breaking the rule," said Indra.

"No, I'm not breaking any rule."

We all took out our papers and showed him that he was not supposed to engage in politics.

"I am not *talking* of politics," he explained. "I'm *listening* to a political discussion."

"We are not lawyers," I said. "You know quite well what we implied by that. You can't get out of this on a technicality."

"Turn it off," said Harsh.

"It's your fault if you did not make explicit what you implied," said Ankit.

"Don't be so obstinate," I said.

"I'm not obstinate."

Indra began to chuckle. Ankit felt he was mocking him (we knew he was). I took the radio and turned it off. Ankit moved his hand to turn it on again, but Harsh made a grab at the radio and took it.

"Give it back to me."

"Not at all."

"On the contrary, you have to undertake some punishment."

"I will do nothing of the sort."

"You will carry water for us the next morning," I said.

"No, I will not."

"We will not let you bathe if you do not do that," said Indra.

It was quite clear that Ankit would have liked to have a go at us, but felt that he was outmatched by Indra alone. The prospect of carrying water was comparatively far too economical and physically advantageous.

"All right," he said, as if he'd decided to do something which we were not willing to do.

I noticed a spark in his eyes while he said this, and knew he was up to some not-at-all-serious-but-delaying antic.

The mosquito repellent was no match for the army of mosquitoes that began to attack us. Gulliver was far less pricked by needle-like arrows.[28]

We decided to move back to the tents and plan our next strategy while eating. We all crowded inside one tent.

"The food is outside," said Indra, after he had seated himself comfortably.

I went with Harsh to get the food. Superman would have envied our speed of rushing out and coming back.

"Tempt not a desperate man," was what I would have told him had he asked us how we did it so fast. I would then obviously tell him about the source.[29]

At 10:00p.m., the battle song of the mosquitoes was more than enough for us not to mind them. Our defensive talk – I mean chat – was far surpassed by their jubilant cries. We decided to go to bed. There was no bed – we were to sleep on rugs – for sleeping-bags would cost us a lot.

"I'll sleep with Harsh," said Indra. I'm sure he meant it as he said it, and did not use any euphemism.

"I'll sleep…" began Ankit.

"Yes, that is understood," I cut him short. I did not wish him to finish the sentence.

The night passed peacefully; the one light from one of the Chinese torches soon succumbed to the thronging mosquitoes, and fell down and went out.

The night passed peacefully, except for the howling of wolves, flipping of bats, hooting of the owl, creeping of some creatures (we did not venture to look or guess) and weird noises from the other

---

[28] In his first adventure, Gulliver lands among the Lilliputians, and at first, he is tied by them. When he tries to get up, he is shot at by the little people, and the arrows prick him like needles.

[29] If I did not tell him of the source, I would commit plagiarism. The source is *Romeo and Juliet*.

tent.[30] The rooster roused us with his cry well before we could see the sun (or the rooster) and we could not go to sleep after that.

"Hey, Ankit, are you awake?" I asked.

"I'm sleeping."

"Then how come you are talking?"

"I talk while I sleep."[31]

"Well, I have *not* heard you talk *at all* all through the night."

"That is because you were sleeping."

I am not used to getting cheeks from others, so, after a moment, I said,

"How did *you* know I was sleeping if you were sleeping?"

I have not read Shakespeare or Seneca in vain. Replies could have been made to that question, but they did not come to him. Ankit knew that he was lost, and so offered no reply.

I went out for my morning ablutions. When I came back, Ankit was not to be seen, but could be heard scrapping among the bushes and talking to himself. This was the second rule he had broken. I mean, the second time he had broken the rules.

"I'll teach him to take my radio," he was grumbling. There came the sharp SNAP of breaking a short bamboo stick.

"Now I am armed," he said victoriously. I decided to play a role in this as the Duke had in *Measure for Measure*.[32] I went in the opposite direction and broke a bamboo stick myself and kept it outside the other tent.

---

[30] So, the night actually did not pass peacefully.

[31] This is an allusion to *The Adventures of Tintin: Prisoners of the Sun*, where Captain Haddock rings the phone, and Thompson and Thomson are both awakened by the ringing, but no one wishes to get up. The dialogue between them is similar.

[32] In *Measure for Measure*, the Duke in disguise sees a lot of things, and plans the course of action. I do not take any disguise, but plan things without letting the others know.

V

I was making tea when Harsh came outside, tripped on the stick, and fell. He clutched wildly with his hands to catch one of the ropes that raised the tent. So, the tent fell shortly afterwards.[33]

"What the hell's happening," came the grumbling shout from Indra.

He struggled with the tent, apparently thinking someone was trying to kidnap him (no doubt he was still sleepy to imagine that!). The result was that the other pegs came off, and one fell on his hands.

He was now certain the kidnapper was trying to beat him with a rod, and he fought all the more. Fighting with nobody increases one's strength.

Harsh had got up long before and was enjoying the scene. He had taken the stick in his hand subconsciously.

After ten minutes, Indra emerged from the tent. We hid ourselves in the bushes. He thought the kidnapper had fled, and bravely sat down. We came out when we were sure we could control our laughter.

Tea was ready.

After their morning ablutions, we sat down to breakfast.

"Where's Ant?" asked Indra to Harsh.

"I do not know," I answered, looking at Harsh.

It was a truthful answer. He had removed himself from that place when Indra had begun to shout.

"I think he's gone to fetch water," said Harsh.

"The carrier is still here," I remarked.

After finishing our breakfast, Harsh suggested we play cricket with "this stick as a bat".

"We'll have to field by climbing up trees," said Indra sarcastically.

"You will have use with this stick," I said.

---

[33] This is to be imagined in slow-motion.

Harsh was going to say something, when, at that moment, with a war-like cry, Ankit emerged from the bushes in front of us, and rushed at Harsh with his stick.

Both the sticks were like the sides of Samurai swords.

Harsh picked up his sword and prevented Ankit's strike. Ankit was shocked to see this sword (he evidently thought he possessed the One Elder Stick),[34] but suppressed his shock with anger. Harsh got up, shocked and infuriated. Ankit attacked again.

The two began fencing.

Indra watched the progress while munching chips.

I took photos of this memorable incident.

It was hard to say who was Brad Pitt and who was Antonio Banderas;[35] who was Bond and who was Bourne;[36] who was Yoda and who was the Sith lord;[37] who was Luke Skywalker and who was the Darth Vader.[38]

The desolation it caused was the overturning of the gas cylinder (which was turned off). Finally, both stepped on a rope of the one tent that remained raised and fell down. They fell on the tent and the tent fell on them; the tent was on them and they were on the tent. The stick-like swords (or sword-like sticks) went out of their hands. The battle had ended, and they struggled to get out.

We had quite an entertainment.

Then we realised (or rather, the others realised then) that there was no more food. The tents had fallen. There was no point in fixing them up again. We decided to pack up and head back.

Ankit carried all the packets, papers and tins in his rucksack along with his clothes. Our rucksacks were considerably lessened in weight.

"I've proved my point," said Ankit, just before we left the woods.

---

[34] The allusion is to *Harry Potter and the Deathly Hallows*, where there is supposed to be one Elder wand, which is superior to all the other wands. The use of the One is also an allusion to *The Matrix* trilogy, where Neo is called the One.

[35] The allusion is to *Troy* and *The Mask of Zorro* films.

[36] The allusion is to James Bond movies and the *Bourne* trilogy.

[37] The allusion is to *Star Wars Episode III: Revenge of the Sith*.

[38] The allusion is to *Star Wars: The Return of the Jedi*.

We were instantly reminded of punishing Ankit.

"We are not going without bathing," said Indra.

So, Ankit had to fetch water for us.

After that, we set out. Harsh and Ankit broke the sticks in halves and carried them as mementos.

It was difficult to find an auto with four empty seats, especially as the pujas were still going on. We had to wait for twenty minutes by the side of the road.

Back home, we were flooded by calls from our college friends. Harsh told them about his defending us; Ankit told them how he had finally proved his point that the four of us do not get along with each other.

I told the others all they needed to know.

Indra told all he knew – how he fought with a kidnapper, and advised others not to go to camp.

LAS BELLES SANS MERCI[39]

OR

GIRLS JUST WANNA HAVE FUN[40]

I

The shops of College Street were still not open the day after the Pujas. The college was, however, open (the gate that is) for students love to go to college during the holidays and do a lot of bunks when classes are held. The canteen however, wasn't open. Neither was any of the Common Rooms. The portico was the only place where the girls could gather for their purpose. To an outsider it would seem that the college girls were opening an organization all by themselves.

All the girls of third year English department were present except Sanjukta and Shikha. The rest had all gathered and it need not be told what happens when girls get together.

They giggle.[41]

It was only this giggling that prevented every onlooker (which comprised all the passers-by) from thinking that the girls had any serious plan of setting an organization.

It was 11.30 a.m. After ten more minutes, Sanjukta, the President of the meeting, and Shikha, the Secretary of the meeting, walked in. It is the custom of the President and the Secretary to walk in late.

"Ladies," began Sanjukta, and silence fell among them all. "Thank you for coming on such a short notice of two days' time."

---

[39] The title is an allusion to Keats' poem, *La Belle Dame sans Merci*.

[40] The sub-title is an allusion to the song, *Girls Just Wanna have Fun*.

[41] The allusion is to Harry Potter, where the girls are shown to be characteristically giggling.

Apu was writing the minutes of the meeting.

"The issue is so tempting, Sanjukta," said Sanchari.

"We love to get an upper hand over the boys," said Indira.

"Ever since we heard about the camping trip of the boys, we have been longing to so something similar...or more," said Sanjukta. The others nodded in agreement.

"Harsh told me that he fought off some savage man who was attacking them," said Bishakha, "I cannot let my boyfriend go so far ahead. I must even up with him.'

"Good for you," said Pushpita.

"Ladies," began Sanjukta once more, "I'm so glad to see how unanimous we are in our decision. Yet the world thinks we are our worst enemies.[42] It is time we proved them wrong."

"Yeah," said Devi.

"I'm so glad you have come," said Parnaa to Devi who beamed with joy.

"We propose to go somewhere – all by ourselves – and even up with the boys," said Shikha.

Everybody cheered, except Ananya Mukherjee and Sreetama. Their silence was easily noticed amid the crowd of cheering girls.

"You seem to have something else to say," said Barnali.

"Well, I was wondering if we would be allowed to do such a thing," said Ananya.

"And distance does matter to me," said Sreetama.

"I must thank you for bringing to limelight these two barriers," said Sanjukta. "Parents. Husbands. Boyfriends. Teachers. We are all the time surrounded by them. They do not seem to realise the potential of the 21st century girl. Or perhaps they are afraid that we are going to take over their monarchy. Well, if they put the kettle down and keep sitting on it, they will soon experience the force of being thrown off!"[43]

---

[42] There is a proverb that a girl is a girl's worst enemy. I am disinterested in the proverb.

[43] This is an allusion to *Uncle Tom's Cabin*, where a character states this about the slaves of the US.

"I say let's kick them!" said Indira.

"We will," said Parnaa.

"Ladies," continued Sanjukta, "Throughout history, women have always been subjected to torture and humiliation. But we have always risen up from the Lethe[44] into which the males want to push us, and have rejuvenated like the phoenix[45] and have sung the song of freedom."

"Yeah," came the shout from others.

"They are not going in the right track, are they?" asked Ananya Mukherjee.

"They never do," answered Sreetama.

"We propose going to Nicco Park or Science City or Millennium Park or camping out like the boys," said Katha.

"We will definitely not camp out. It's dangerous," said Barnali.

"Besides, we don't want to do what the boys have done," said Sikha.

"Millennium Park sounds good," said Alolika.

"We will not like it there," said Adrija, "I've been there."

"Science City should be a nice treat," said Pushpita.

"It's really expensive," said Barnali.

"Our parents will not give us such an amount," said Devi.

"Well, then we are going to Nicco Park," said Divya.

"Yeah," said everybody.

"Nicco Park's fine with me," said Ananya.

"Me too!" said Sreetama.

"After the Oxford Movement, it is now time for the 21st century Presidency Movement," said Sara.

"We have always led others. Let the movement begin!" said Sanjukta.

"Yeah," came the resounding reply.

The few stalls that had opened in this while hurriedly made preparations to shut themselves again, fearing demonstrations by hearing the unanimous reply.

It is a known fact that girls' voices are shriller than boys.

---

[44] Lethe is the river of forgetfulness in Greek mythology.

[45] Phoenix is a mythical bird that lives for a thousand years, burns itself on a pyre, and rises from its own ashes.

"So when do we go?" asked Maya.

There was some murmuring at this, which obviously resulted in another round of giggling.

"How about...hee, hee…this Sunday," squeaked Kankana.

"That sounds perfect," said Shikha.

"Me too," said Barnali "Hee, hee".

"Me too," said Poulami.

"Count me in, too," said Panchali.

"Me too," said Shobha.

"Count in all of us," said Ankita.

"YEAH!"

The stalls which were fooled into opening by hearing the laughter were all quickly shut again.

"So, have we come to this unanimous decision that we go to Nicco park this Sunday?" asked Sanjukta.

"Yeah!"

"When shall we meet?" asked Sreetama.[46]

"10.00 a.m."

"No, it's too early for me. Make it 11.00 a.m."

"That will be too late," said Barnali.

"Then let's meet at 10.35 a.m." suggested Sara.

"Yeah."

"Where the place?" asked Pushpita.

"At the Park's gate," said Shikha.

"There we will rub our hands with clays," said Urbashi.

"For what, dear?" asked Pushpita.

"My hands are slippery. I need to grip the handle-bars tightly while on the rides."

"You can rub some powder," suggested Kankana.

"Yeah, but that does not rhyme with 'place'."

---

[46] The following lines are a parody of the opening lines of *Macbeth*.

"Oh yeah," said Barnali.
"Yeah!"

The stall-owners were thinking of going home.
"Boys end their discussions so soon," said one of them. "These girls go on and on."

"So, we meet in front of Nicco Park's gate at 10.35a.m., this Sunday," said Sanjukta.
"Yeah!"
"I was thinking of 'Hooray'."
"HOORAY!"
"That's better. Thank you for coming here," said Sanjukta.

Everyone got up, giggled and left. The stall-owners were about to leave when they saw the girls go. They came back.
The stall-owners embraced each other and ordered sweets.
The girls went as fast as they could and waited for Sunday.

II

All the girls were assembled in front of the gate well before time. This time, Sanjukta was the first to arrive. The others all arrived soon, except Sreetama, who arrived at 10.25 a.m.
"Well," said Indira," what are we waiting for? Let's kick some asses!"
"Yeah!"
"Charge!" shouted Sanjukta.
"YEAH!"
So they all went inside, Sanjukta leading them. All eyes turned towards them, all bodies moved away from them. A few boys who dared to smile in an erotic manner were instantly aware of their stupidity, for they were met with looks that would turn a gorgon into a stone.[47]

---

[47] A gorgon was a mythological creature which had heads of snakes instead of hair, and anyone who looked at the creature was turned into stone.

"We'd like twenty six bands, please," said Sanjukta at the ticket counter. These bands enabled them to have all the rides as many times as they could. The price was obviously considerably low, in consideration of the great thrill of the rides.

They first chose the mild, quiet, paddling boat.
Soon, the lake was filled with girls racing against each other, swearing and sweating. Various boys lined up and on the jetty and placed bets.

"Now we are giving them something," shouted Bishakha.
"Yeah."
"Don't you wish your girlfriends could paddle like us," jeered Sanchari to the boys in a sing-song voice.[48]
The boys just looked on.
Ananya and Sreetama came last in the race, because Ananya could not paddle so well.
"Don't cry," consoled Sreetama, "well get the better of them in striking cars."

And sure enough, Ananya's force did kick some cars out and the rest were afraid to come near theirs.
"Wheeee!" said Ananya, as she turned the car around and hit Divya and Devi.
"Oohh," said Devi.
"Aahh," said Divya.
The two girls' car bumped into Poulami's and Bishakha's car.
"Ouch," said the two of them.
"Ha, ha," said Maya.
"You Tom boy," said Bishakha, "Why don't you hit Ananya?"
So Maya, greatly flattered by the praise and instigated at the prospect of glory, searched around for Ananya and Sreetama.
"Where are they?" she said aloud.

---

[48] This is an allusion to the pop song *Don't cha*, one of whose lines is, "Don't you wish your girlfriend was hot like me?"

"Right behind you," shouted a voice. Maya turned around – no, not the car, just her head – and saw Ananya's grin, spreading wider and coming nearer. The wild terror of defeat flashed in her eyes, and her Tom Boyish nature made her move aside just in time.

"Scared of us?" jeered Sreetama.

At this, Maya resolved not to hit them.

"Never hit girls," she said laughingly. It was not clear whether she was using the popular men's saying to justify her resolve or out of defense.

"Too bad for you," said Ananya, "'Cause in that way we can hit on."

She drove their car straight at Maya and Maya's car went sliding to the other corner.

The bell rang, and the round was over. Ananya emerged as the champion, Sreetama as her trainer.

It was decided that their victory should be celebrated by eating, so the girls made their way to ransack the restaurant of its food. They had to occupy seats before others. Shikha, Pushpita, Sara and Adrija made their way towards a table with four chairs, when they were angered at seeing four boys approaching from the other side, who evidently made for the same seats. The girls ran.

The boys walked, for they were a few steps away from the table.

The boys were comfortably seated for a minute before the girls came up.

"These are our seats," said Adrija.

The boys looked at them and began to laugh and converse in a language that the girls could not comprehend.

"They must be talking about us," said Pushpita.

"Are you taking about us?" asked Adrija.

One of the boys looked up.

"Yes, we are," he said, "Any problem with that? If you have, you are welcome to sit elsewhere where you can't hear us."

"These are our seats and we won't go," said Sara.

"I don't see any names written on these," said another boy.

"Neither do we," said Sara. "So we will not go."

"Cool," said another guy in an erotic tone.

Katha placed her hands on the table so that the boy could see it.

"Look," she began, "you do not want to sit here."

"We…we do not want to sit here," said one boy, looking at the hand.[49]

"You want to get up and buy us some drinks."

"We want to get up and buy you some drinks," said another boy.

They got up and went away. The girls took their seats.

"How did you do that?" asked Adrija.

"Well," said Shikha, "If OB1 can do it in a galaxy far, far away,[50] there's no reason why we can't do it here. We just need to charm them."

 "Cool," said Pushpita.

III

It was decided that they would ride the cable-car next. The steps leading to it would give them exercise and the fresh air would fill their minds with noble ideas of how to conquer the boys. Breathing in the fresh air can generate such pure thoughts. So, with sublime and graceful steps, the girls went up the stairs, the cries of others in the queue passing out from their ears, for their minds were on higher things. There was just one barrier to be thrown down if they were to reach the summit – the person in charge of the cable-car.[51]

"Hey, can't you see the queue, ladies?" he asked.

"First," said Sanchari.

The person was obviously not used to such wits.

---

[49] This part is an allusion to *Star Wars Episode II*, where OB1 makes a creature do his bidding by waving his hand and speaking to him.

[50] Reference to the Star Wars, where one can control the minds of lesser animals easily.

[51] This is to be taken figuratively.

"Ladies first," explained Barnali.

"That's not what I meant," began the man.

"Apology accepted," said Sanjukta. "Now excuse us. We see that a cable car has arrived."

"Wait…no," said the man, rushing towards her. But Sanjukta had already taken charge of things.

She gave the man a quick slap.

"Be careful," she said.

"What the… are you mad?"

"I will file a report against you. Trying to rush at me in public! Are you in league with the bus conductors?"[52]

The man was about to say something, but Sanjukta silenced him with another wave of her hand. The boy who was in front of the queue – a muscular guy – came up to his aid.

"Hey, girls, what do you think you are doing?"

"Watch instead of asking!" snapped Shikha.

"I merely asked 'cause you blockheads don't seem to realise by looking at me that I am stronger than any of you!"

He took two steps forward.

Click! Click!

The boy turned sideways. Alolika and Adrija were holding their camera phones[53] and smiling.

"We've taken your picture and will give it to the press if you advance any more," said Alolika.

"I've also recorded your words. They can be interpreted in various ways," said Adrija, and she stepped inside the cable car that had arrived. Alolika went in after her. Parnaa and Pushpita followed.

"So, if you do not want further trouble," said Katha, "back off!"

---

[52] At that time, there were quite a few reports about ladies being harassed by bus conductors. Readers should note that the Delhi rape incident (December 2012) had not yet taken place at that time, and no insult is meant to the victim of that unfortunate event, or other such events.

[53] Back when this was written, not all mobiles had cameras. The ones which had were called "camera phones".

The boy did take a few steps backwards. The man-in-charge was standing, rubbing his cheeks. By this time others – who were in front of the queue – had come up after the boy.

"Ladies," shouted Sanjukta, "It's time you took things in your hands. How long will you wait here in the queue for boys and men to lead you? Step up."

 "Yeah!"

A few girls did step up, and there was a lot of cheering. Those who were below obviously thought everything was normal and didn't seem bothered by the fact that the crowd of girls who had walked past them was slowly diminishing. As long as someone cheered and nobody in front complained, things were fine.

So, the girls had a wonderful ride on the cable cars. Their minds were blown upwards by the recent jubilation, and they were all laughing. None of them were in the least bothered.

Water-chute came next, followed by the River Cave Ride. By then, news of the girls had spread to every man in-charge of a ride, with lots of exaggeration. The result was that the girls were given special treatment, and the laughter that rang through them would have brought a fairy to listen to them and bless them for their innocence.

Poulami was immensely bored with the River Cave Ride, while Ananya wanted to have another go. However, the majority were for Simuthriller,[54] for they felt River Cave Ride was far less thrilling, and wanted to experience the thrill of this new ride. However, they found the ride to be pretty similar to that of boys' games, and were bored.

"Let's go conquer the moon," said Indira.

"What?" asked Barnali.

"I think she means moon raker," said Sayoni.

"Oh, yes," said Manshi, "Let's go to the moon."

---

[54] The name of this ride has now been changed.

"I have heard it is not that good," said Barnali.

"My friends say that the only good part is that you have to shout," said Sara.

"That too, is out of convention," said Pushpita, "Besides, there is no other fun."

"I haven't been to that ride," said Indira.

"Me neither," said Sanchari.

"We should go to that 'whirl' thing," suggested Bishakha.

"What?" asked Sanjukta.

"Those half-open eggs," said Bishakha, "with people inside."

She understood the joke after she had uttered it, and quickly corrected it. All the others were giggling.

"I mean, the ones that have 'E-----' written on them."[55]

"The former explanation was better," said Sanchari.

"The second leads to a lot of speculation," observed Poulami.

"So what do you think?"

"I want to ride the moon raker!" said Shobha.

"I want to be inside that thing marked 'E-----'."

"I say we go to the moon," said Panchali.

"No, spinning inside that thing is definitely more fun."

"Let's split," said Sanjukta.

"No, we must remain united," said Barnali.

"I meant for the ride," replied Sanjukta.

"Oh," said Barnali.

"It's a good idea," said Katha. "The ones who want to go to the Moon Raker, go, and the ones who want to come to this thing marked 'E-----', let's go!"

"That is brilliant," said Manshi.

"I shall always remember this wonderful distinction between 'go' and 'come' in this sentence," said Urbashi.

So, the ten girls, who wish to remain unnamed (those who have already shown their desire are included), went to ride on moon raker. The rest, who wish to remain unnamed also (though some have already disclosed their preferences), went to have a whirl.

---

[55] These were labeled 'Eveready'. These labels are no longer there, and the name of the ride has been changed.

Both parties wish to remain unnamed because both were embarrassed. The former group was embarrassed as they saw that the others were right about that ride, and so, do not wish to reveal themselves. The latter group was embarrassed because all of them were subjected to head-spinning or vomiting. While riding, each group wished they had taken the other ride; after comparing the results, they wished they had never gone for any of them.

IV

Flying Saucer suffered a terrible blow, as the girls decided to leave it out. The man-in-charge was, however, greatly relieved to see them hurriedly pass by. He expressed his jubilation openly.
"Unmannered fellow, no sense of decency at all," said Parnaa.
"Very unfeeling," said Kankana.
"Let's take the roller coaster ride," said Katha.
"I'm hungry," said Kankana, "My stomach's so empty."
"Yes," said Pushpita, "looking at my watch, I see it's 4.00p.m. When did the time pass?"
"In rides," said Barnali.
"Well said," said Sara.

So, the girls went to have some snacks, after which they decided to experience the roller coaster ride.
"Our teachers, I mean, one of our teachers in school, said that there's a free-fall of thirty-two feet," said Urbashi.
"Oh, and which subject did he take?" asked Barnali.
"Well, he took one of the commerce subjects," said Urbashi. "So, I have never been taught by him, I just heard him say so once."[56]
"He does not know what a free-fall is," said Barnali. "This is not a free-fall. We're rolling down the rails at an inclined angle – and there's obviously resistance imposed by machines and wires. In

---

[56] This remark was actually made by a teacher in my school. No disrespect is meant towards the teacher or the subject. It is only for the sake of clarification that is mentioned.

free-fall, there is simply a drop-down – and the only resistance is offered by air."

"Well, *he* certainly did not know that," remarked Urbashi.

The man-in-charge took a look at the approaching girls and let them ride on. It took two rounds for all of them to ride on it.

"Hold me tightly," said Ananya to Sreetama.

"Hold the handle-bars, silly," said Sreetama.

"No, you please hold me, otherwise I will be afraid."

"If I hold you, *I'll* be afraid."

The ride started.

"Yeah!" screamed some girls.

"Ooohh!" screamed some other girls.

"Aaaaahh!" screamed Ananya, closing her eyes.

"Will you stop it?" shouted Sreetama. "We're just going up! You need to scream when we roll down."

"Here we go," said Kankana.

"Yeeeaaaah!"

"Ooohh!"

"Aaaaahhhh!" screamed Ananya, closing her eyes.

"EEEEKK!" screamed Adrija.

Ananya stopped screaming to look at her but shut her eyes instantly.

"EEEEEEKKKKKK! Stop the ride! Stop the ride!" said Adrija.

So, the man in-charge stopped the ride and Adrija got out. Pushpita followed.

"I am so sorry," said Pushpita.

"Sorry?" said Adrija. "You must be crazy! Why did you bring that hot coffee with you on the ride?[57] Didn't you know it would spill out? And look at my dress! It's all stained!"

---

[57] It must be clarified that nothing of this sort would be allowed in these rides. But that would not do for the story, so I have inserted this, without meaning to show negligence on part of the men in-charge of such rides. Moreover, it's an allusion to a soft drink advertisement, where a person takes the soft drink on a roller coaster ride, and it does not spill out, for he keeps turning it when the vehicle turns. However, when a girl asks him for telling the time, he turns his hand to look at his wrist-watch, and the drink spills out.

"I am so sorry."

"What were you thinking?"

"I was just trying to mimic that advertisement. Maya said she'd shoot it on her handy-cam. Well, she could not take out her handy-cam, but I had the coffee cup. The man in-charge did not bother to bother us – they are all scared after what we did with that man in-charge of the cable cars."

"You spoiled my dress!"

"I am so sorry. Let me compensate. Here – have my cup of coffee." Adrija glared at her, and took the cup. Pushpita felt she'd sip it, but Adrija just threw it on her.

"Are you out of your mind?" said Pushpita to a laughing Adrija.

"Now we're even. Let's go back and ride."

Pushpita felt betrayed, but followed, for she certainly did not wish to let go of the ride.

All the girls were too hot after the ride, so they felt they would chill out on the fake snow.

Pushpita took some great shots at Adrija with snow balls, who was too cold[58] to be angry with her.

"Let's have some snacks," suggested Sanchari.

"We just had some," said Barnali.

"So? There's no rule that we can't eat again, is there?"

"You are right," said Indira.

"Yeah!"

Over the steaming cups of coffee, tea, soft drinks, ice-creams and biscuits, the girls sat and discussed.

It obviously began with giggles.

---

[58] There is a pun on this word. On the one hand, I mean that as she was being pelted with snowballs, she felt too cold. On the other hand, I mean that she was still a bit cold (hostile) from the incident at the roller coaster ride.

"It's 5.00p.m." said Barnali, after the formality was over. "We should be heading home."

"Yeah, I told my parents I'd be back by 6.35 p.m." said Kankana.

"My… you know who… will wait for me," said Ankita.

"My jethu[59] will come to pick me up," said Ananya. "I must call him up right now." She began to speed-dial her home and talk to her mother.

"We had great fun," said Barnali.

"Of course," said Sara.

"We have showed the boys we can do things," said Sanjukta.

"Yeah!"

"But *he* will be waiting for me. I have to go, too," continued Sanjukta.

Bishakha sighed.

"Whazup?" asked Maya.

"Well, I just wish Harsh could see me here."

Several of the girls sighed.

"I just wish the boys were with us," said Poulami.

"Yeah!" sighed the others.

"We would definitely have had more fun watching them tackle things, thinking they are doing us big favours," said Shikha.

"They would have tried to lead us, thinking we are incapable, and not at all guessing that we want them to lead us, while we follow leisurely," said Kankana.[60]

"We would have loved to see Indra paddling on one of those boats!" remarked Sanchari.

"Yeah!"

Ananya finished talking and told Sreetama that her jethu would come within twenty-five minutes.

"How long do we have to stay here?" asked Sreetama to Shobha.

"We will obviously not go out before 5.35p.m.," she replied. "We still have to fill out bottles with water from there," she pointed.

"Oh," said Ananya, relieved. "It's all right then."

---

[59] Uncle who is an elder brother to the father.

[60] This is to be taken humorously. I certainly do not wish to state that girls have this tendency (other than their tendency of being wooed).

"Hey girls," said Katha, "I have a toast."

They all raised up their coffee, soft drinks, tea or ice-creams.

"To a wonderful time," said Katha.

"To a wonderful time," chimed in the others.

"And wishing the boys were here and proposing to go out with them the next time."

"Yeah!"

"To us!"

"To us!"

"Cheers"! said everybody and giggled.

"Imagine Harsh or Ankit fighting for us with that muscular guy and that cable car in-charge," said Bishakha.

"Hee, hee, hee, hee" giggled everybody.

So, the evening went on; they finished their snacks, filled up their bottles and went outside. Ananya's jethu was standing there.

"We've had a nice time," said Sanjukta.

"Yeah!"

"Hey!" said Ananya, "I think I'll tell Saheb to write this as a story for us."

"That would be great," seconded Sreetama.

"Yeah!"

Almost all cell-phones began to ring just then. They were either from the girls' homes or from their boyfriends. So, they all hurriedly decided to go, entrusting Ananya to tell Saheb to pen the incident as a story.

"I can't wait to read this story on the empowerment of women," said Sanjukta.

ALL IN A DAY'S WORK

It was raining heavily. Barnali was crying bitterly. She had scored only 90% in her university exams. University of Calcutta. Known internationally[61] for its stringent marking scheme.[62]

"BOOO-HOOO! I'm not worthy!" She wailed, her tears falling on the printed mark sheet.

Kankana, sitting by her side on the corridor, could only mouth the words of cold consolation of stupefaction,

"It's unbelievable!"

"I know! How can I look at myself in the mirror?"

Kankana had no answer to that. She just looked at the pouring rain, wondering how she would reach home to tell that she had got a first class. In a few minutes, Pushpita arrived, with a paper cup of soft-drinks. Evidently, she had been to the canteen to celebrate her first class.

"Congratulations, Barnali…" she began, when a glaring Kankana shot arrows from her eyes to shut her mouth.

Thankfully, Barnali had not heard the first part. Pushpita sat down, looking at Barnali with a visible lack of comprehension as to the reason of her tears.

"What's the matter with her?" She asked Kankana.

"I have got 90%!" sobbed Barnali.

"Only," added Kankana, as an explanation.

Pushpita opened her mouth to say something, but there was a flash of lightning, followed by more rain and tears.

---

[61] Various universities abroad had listed on their websites that because of the stringent marking scheme of Calcutta University, they are willing to lower the marks requirement of students who apply from Calcutta University. This is stated not as a defamatory statement, but as a fact. Sadly, not all other places are so considerate, and often, the students suffer.

[62] The highest that is given in the language and the arts is in the range of 60%, awarded to less than a handful of students from all colleges combined.

As each thought how to console Barnali and make her see the reasoning sun in the midst of cloudy rain, a distant rumbling was heard. As it became louder, it turned to a grumbling, and soon, the source appeared. It was Ankit who came round the corner, with a cup of coffee in his hand, talking non-stop to no one. He came and sat down.

"Coffee?" he asked, stopping his flow of words to the invisible person, and addressing the visible friends.
"Coffee is not my cup of tea," said Pushpita.[63]
"What's that in your hand?" asked Ankit
"Soft-drinks. Can't you see?" snapped Pushpita.
"Do you know this is bad for your health?"

Barnali stopped crying because she was really surprised that Ankit did not even notice that she was crying. Ankit continued.
"These are pesticides. You should not drink them."
"Well, coffee is not very healthy either, unlike tea," said Pushpita.
"Aha! Coffee is bad if taken in excess."
"So are soft-drinks bad if taken in excess. A cup does not harm."
"O ho, ho! It does. A cup also contains the same harmful things."
"A cup of coffee also carries the same harmful things."
Ankit got up in excitement. Barnali watched him.
"Aha," he continued, "coffee has caffeine. It makes the brain wake up, so to speak. If taken in excess, it causes harm to the liver and might also cause insomnia. So, a cup of coffee does not harm."
"Aha," mimicked Pushpita, "a cup of soft-drinks has lots of sugar, which is good for instant energy. A lot would harm, but not a cup."
"I do not agree," said Ankit.
"I beg to differ with your disagreement," said Pushpita, gulping down the remaining portion of the liquid, and throwing the empty cup into a gutter.
"Why don't you two just shut up," said Kankana.

---

[63] This is an allusion to George Bernard Shaw's words, where he expressed something similar.

She was unheeded, for Ankit was furious at Pushpita's action, and could not remain a silent spectator.

"How dare you throw it there and dirty the gutter?" he said.

"I had no idea the gutters were meant to be kept clean."

Ankit became red with anger.

"You have no concern for your health or the environment. You should throw it in a dustbin!"

"I don't see any dustbin here."

"There is one in the canteen."

"You expect me to go all the way to the canteen just to throw this?"

"Then you should put this inside your bag and carry it about with you, and throw it inside a dustbin when you reach home or a dustbin."

"And make my bag a haunted house of ants?"

"You don't understand!" roared Ankit.

"Look," said Kankana, who was again unheeded.

"I will not stand this!" said Ankit, and began walking towards the gutter, finishing his coffee.

"I will certainly not put it inside my bag if you put it out of the gutter," said Pushpita, with a clear foresight of what Ankit intended to do.

"This is a bio-degradable product, this cup!" said Barnali. All looked at her. "Why don't you just let it go? She has thrown it inside the gutter, not on the street!"

"But it will block the gutter!"

"No, it won't! It will soften and will not obstruct the flow of water, but will deteriorate. And as it is a bio-degradable product, it will not harm the environment. So, why don't you just let it go?"

Ankit was silent. He looked at the cup in his hand.

"All right," he said. I will let it go. But I will not throw my cup into the gutter. I will put it inside the dustbin in the canteen."

"Please suit yourself," said Kankana.

So, Ankit left, conversing again with his invisible companion.

"So, where were we before he came?" said Kankana.

"I have no idea," said Barnali.

"I think we were celebrating the fact that you have got the highest," said Pushpita, in a flash of wit.

"Oh really? WOW!" exclaimed Barnali. "I feel like crying!"

PLAYS

We Think

Therefore

You Are[64]

(A Comedy in Five Acts)

---

[64] The title is an allusion to Descartes' statement, "Cogito, ergo sum" (I think, therefore I am).

Act I

Scene I: The Lounge

Enter Parnaa and Alolika from right, and sit on the sofas.

PARNAA: We are really early.

ALOLIKA: Yes, this is the first time we are so early![65]

PARNAA: I cannot believe there is no one to whom we can tell the record news.

ALOLIKA: If there was someone before us, we could not have made the record.

PARNAA: Well, maybe we wouldn't have been the first ones, but we would still have been early.

ALOLIKA: That's true.

PARNAA: *[Reclining]* Oh, I'm so happy. Wait, there is something here *[she gets up and removes the cushion]*. A note book.

ALOLIKA: Let me see.

Parnaa gives her the note book.

                        There is no name here. *[She turns the pages; Parnaa bends over to see.]*

PARNAA: What are these things?

---

[65] In the UG days, these two girls were reputed for never turning up for the first class.

ALOLIKA: Words, words, words![66] But I can't make out any word.

PARNAA: It must be a code language.

ALOLIKA: That is it! It is obviously a code language!

Footsteps are heard.

PARNAA: Someone's coming. Quick, hide the book.

Alolika finds nowhere to hide the book. She sits down on it. Enter Archita and Divya from right.

DIVYA: Hello!

ALOLIKA: [*Getting up*] I'm so glad it's you. We've found this! Look! *She throws the note book; there is a great fuss over it.*

PARNAA: It's a secret. Do not tell anyone. We do not know who the person is.

ARCHITA: What do you think the person is up to?

DIVYA: We have to decipher the code to find that out.

Voices heard within.

                  Quick! Hide the book.

The book is in Archita's hands. She finds nowhere to hide the book. She sits down, the note book in her hands.

PARNAA: Hide it!

---

[66] An allusion to *Hamlet.*

ARCHITA:	I can't find a place. I'll just pretend that it is mine.

Enter Adrija from right.

ADRIJA:	I shouted and I shouted! You two – are you deaf? Never heard a syllable!
ARCHITA:	Was it you who was shouting like that?
ADRIJA:	You heard me?
DIVYA:	Of course! Everyone at Central Metro Station heard it.
ADRIJA:	Why didn't you turn and look?
ARCHITA:	Well, your words were not at all distinctive. You shouted so much that we thought someone was calling for some sort of political agitation at zero hour's notice! So, we hurried on.
ADRIJA:	WHAT?!
DIVYA:	Besides, it was only yesterday that Prof. _____ was telling us that we Indians look for every source of noise even though it does not concern us.[67] That is why we did not turn around.
ADRIJA:	I cannot believe it!
DIVYA:	We are so sorry! We'll look back the next time.
ADRIJA:	Next time? I cannot believe it! I run and I shout for a couple of girls who walk in comfort and do not bother to turn their

---

[67] No Professor said this, but this is an observed fact. There is of course no shadow of racism.

heads, and sit here comfortably in the lounge with bags by their sides, and that note book in hand…what is that note book?

ARCHITA: It's mine.

ADRIJA: Such a haughty reply! No warming up! Well,

I'll snatch it from you.

She makes a grab at the note book. Both girls pull at it.

ALOLIKA: Stop it! You will tear the note book.

ADRIJA: What is that to you? As for me, I will feel revenged, that is, be avenged!

PARNAA: That is not her note book!

Adrija stops struggling and stares at Parnaa; Archita is thrown backwards on the sofa by her own force.

ARCHITA: Now that Parnaa has spilled the beans, you can see it. Here – [*She gives the book to Adrija.*]

ADRIJA: My, my! What are these?

ALOLIKA: Words, words, words.

PARNAA: We believe it's a code of some sort.

ADRIJA: You are very, very right. But whose could it be?

PARNAA: It must belong to someone from our batch, no doubt.

PARNAA: You mean a college student?

ALOLIKA:	Not just any college student – *our* college student – *our* department – *our* batch.
ADRIJA:	But how can you be so sure?
PARNAA:	Well, other college students do not come to *this* place. They do not know of it. They stay in the canteen.
DIVYA:	Other students – of other departments – do not come here. They do not get a chance, as we sit here all the time the place is open. They used to try at first, but they do not come now.
ARCHITA:	We can safely rule out the PG students – they would write in Greek and Latin. Besides, they are too busy with their term papers to do something so interestingly captivating.
PARNAA:	We can rule out the first years – they are too scared of college life still. It will be some more months before they behave like monkeys.
DIVYA:	I don't think you are right about the first years. Their ego has great potential to display itself in scribbling all over the newly painted college walls.
PARNAA:	Yes. So, even if they do write, it will be in posters, leaflets, or by colouring the walls of the college.

Adrija nods.

| PARNAA: | We can also rule out the lethargic second years. They are obviously not interested in such stuff. |

ADRIJA: You are right. But who can it be?

                     [*Adrija's cell phone rings.*] A text message.
                     [*She reads.*] Class in Room No. 23. [*To the
                     others*] Why do they keep changing the
                     allotted rooms?

ALOLIKA: You'll win the Nobel Prize if you find out.
                     [*They get up.*] I'll keep the note book. [*She
                     takes it.*] Let's go.

Exeunt omnes from right. Lights fade out.

Scene II: The Arts Library

Enter Barnali and Kankana from right.

BARNALI: A spy? Writing in code languages?

KANKANA: Well, they always write in code languages.

BARNALI: Sorry for the mistake.

KANKANA: Don't be. I'm not Ankit.

Enter Ankit from right.

BARNALI: Hi! We were just talking about you.

ANKIT: Oh, and what were you saying?

KANKANA: We can't tell you.

ANKIT: I surely hope you do not think I am any
                     secret agent?

BARNALI: How did you know about the note book?

ANKIT:	Girls can't keep any secret which should be kept, and keep all that inside which they should tell.
KANKANA:	That is a very good figure of speech. So, what do you think?
ANKIT:	I also think it is a very good figure of speech.
BARNALI:	No! We mean about the spy – writing in a code language.
ANKIT:	Well, spies write in code languages only.
BARNALI:	My mistake. I am sorry.
ANKIT:	You should be.

Kankana and Barnali exchange grins.

KANKANA:	So, what do you think about the spy thing?
ANKIT:	What about it?
BARNALI:	Well, whom do you suspect?
ANKIT:	I am sure it is either Indra or Harsh. I have rightly analysed the situation.
KANKANA:	You are just telling their names out of prejudice.
ANKIT:	You should always speak out your prejudices.
BARNALI:	But you must not blame anyone just because you do not like the person.
ANKIT:	You should not blame people you like. So, you should point your finger at those who you dislike.

[*Aside*] I'm really not sure whether it will be "who" or "whom" here. But I am sure they have not noticed it.

KANKANA: When you point a finger at someone, three fingers point at you.

ANKIT: You must not neglect the minority opinion.

BARNALI: The odd ones must be kept out, not in.

ANKIT: Little drops of water make the ocean.

KANKANA: A drop of oil in water does not mix.

ANKIT: Oh, it does, in preparing jhol!

BARNALI: [*Aside*] Now I've got him! [*To Ankit*] Over there, you heat them. The heat loosens the electronic bonding of the atoms, and that is why they appear to mix. After it is cooled, you will see the drops of oil floating on top of the jhol.

ANKIT: [*Aside*] Lost to two girls! But I will fight on.

[*To Barnali*] You are taking advantage of my ignorance.

KANKANA: It would be folly to take advantage of your advantage.

BARNALI: You must always strike at other's drawbacks if you want to win the battle.

ANKIT: [*Aside*] Well and truly beaten! But I will fight on. I am always right. [*To the two girls*] It is cowardly to strike when the opposition's arms have fallen, or when his back is turned.

BARNALI:	Such an ideal was one of the reasons why the Rajputs lost the Battle of Tarain, and for your loss now.
KANKANA:	Never underestimate the power of girls.

Enter Saheb from right.

ANKIT:	Finally! Now it's two boys and two girls. [*To Saheb*] Tell me. Is it "You should point a finger at those who you dislike"?
SAHEB:	No! You shouldn't point your finger if you can help it.

The girls laugh. Ankit is taken aback.

ANKIT:	You should have come a little earlier. I just lost a debate to two girls!
SAHEB:	You should not debate or argue if you can help it, and certainly not with girls!
KANKANA:	See? Saheb acknowledges our power.
SAHEB:	Of course I do! It's preferable to stay away from lionesses.
KANKANA:	Are you calling us beasts?
SAHEB:	Take it as you want it. It's your call. The card is in your hands.
BARNALI:	We prefer not to take it.
SAHEB	It is not wise to refuse your chance. By doing so, you acknowledge defeat.
BARNALI:	It isn't fair!
ANKIT:	All's fair in love and war!

KANKANA: What? You acknowledge that you are either in love with us, or you are a misogynist?

ANKIT: I…I…that is not what I meant.

SAHEB: Well, Ankit lost to you, and you lost to me.

BARNALI: It never even began!

SAHEB: You can see the complete picture only when you are out of it. You refused to pick up your cards. That shows surrender.

KANKANA: [*Consolingly*] At least, we won over Ankit.

SAHEB: So, what do you think about the spy?

KANKANA: How did you know about that?

SAHEB: Ankit told me.

BARNALI: Well, even boys can't keep secrets.

ANKIT: It is not a secret for us.

Enter Sara from right.

             She is the only girl who can keep secrets.

SARA: Thanks for the compliment. By the way, it's really not a secret any more, as everyone knows it, don't they?

BARNALI: Pushpita and Katha don't. Katha's out of town for that poetry competition. Devi,

Manshi and Sayoni are obviously not in touch.[68]

SAHEB: Ananya and Sreetama do not know about it. But I will tell them.

BARNALI: You shouldn't do that!

SAHEB: We told you we boys don't treat this as a secret. Besides, I do not think anybody's spying here, except reporters.[69] You must keep this out of their reach.

KANKANA: Of course.

BARNALI: But you do not think any secret agent has done this?

SAHEB: No, I do not think so.

ANKIT: You are talking like an idiot. I have analysed the situation correctly.

BARNALI: You and your prejudice! But Saheb, what about the strange words of the note book? They are a code of some sort.

SAHEB: I wish you would let me have a look at it.

BARNALI: No. Girls found it; girls keep it.

SAHEB: Very well. I have to go now. Keep chatting.

Exit Saheb from right.

BARNALI: We must find out who the spy is.

---

[68] The three of them hardly attended classes, although they were seen regularly in the canteen.

[69] Presidency was, and still is, a site for reporters. In our five years over there, we would frequently spot them talking with a student or two, seeking stories and making news when there was none.

Enter Adrija from right, running.

ADRIJA: There you are! Listen, I know who the spy is!

THE REST: [*Shouting*] WHO?

Enter Hirak da from left.

HIRAK DA: You girls and boy, you are speaking too loudly. The ones in the reading room are getting disturbed. Please stay quietly, or go outside.

ANKIT: [*Whispering*] We are really sorry. We'll keep it down.

HIRAK DA: Do not mumble! I can't hear you. Speak louder.

ANKIT: [*Normally*] We are really sorry. We'll keep it down.

Exit Hirak Da, grumbling.

SARA: Who is it?

ADRIJA: It's Pushpita!

ANKIT: You must be mistaken. It is either Indra or Harsh. I have analysed the situation correctly.

BARNALI: Pushpita! Unbelievable!

ADRIJA: She called me!

KANKANA: Does she want you to go and keep the note book somewhere so that she can collect it?

ADRIJA:	No! She doesn't even know we have found it. She called me to tell that she has lost a valuable note book and cannot find it in her house.
ANKIT:	That is because it is not in her house. It is here.
KANKANA:	Be quiet. Let her continue.
ADRIJA:	She asked me to search for it in college, and to tell all of you to search for it.
SARA:	She was such a good friend of mine. How she deceived me!
ANKIT:	She must be working under Indra or Harsh.
ADRIJA:	Oh no! It's her note book. The description matches with the one we have found.
KANKANA:	Let's tell the news to the others.

Exeunt. Lights fade out.

Act II

Scene I: Room No. 23

Enter Alolika and Parnaa from left.

ALOLIKA:	Two days in a row, and no one to congratulate us!
PARNAA:	These people enter so late. In a way, it's good, for we get the time to comb our hair.

She takes out a comb.

ALOLIKA:	But your hair is all set.

PARNAA: Oh! [*She keeps the comb inside.*] I carry it all the time with me. As for you, I hope you are carrying the note book safely?

ALOLIKA: Of course! You know that.

PARNAA: Yes, I know. That is why I'll keep saying it, for I am jealous that you are keeping it.

ALOLIKA: Huh?

PARNAA: I found it first!

ALOLIKA: Don't let's get into silly arguments.

PARNAA: Oh, it's always silly when it comes to me, is it not?

ALOLIKA: Parnaa, don't start like a child!

PARNAA: Oh, and you think you are my mother?

ALOLIKA: I didn't mean that!

PARNAA: You always behave as if you are more matured, while I present myself in contrast as a fun-loving immature girl. You do it deliberately. You acted in the same manner so that the others will trust you with the note book.

ALOLIKA: Don't be silly! I'll give it to you if you want it so badly.

PARNAA: Well, you are still not giving it to me.

ALOLIKA: [*Opening her bag and taking out the note book*] Here. Take it and let nothing come between our friendship again.

Parnaa takes the note book and brings it down on Alolika's head.

ALOLIKA: AAW! What was that for?

PARNAA: That was for falling into failure. How could you give it to me?

ALOLIKA: But you only wanted it!

PARNAA: I was pretending! It was planned by a few of us to see if you could be persuaded to give up the note book. You failed easily.

ALOLIKA: [*Innocently*] Oh, OK! I'll never give it to anyone again.

PARNAA: See that you don't. [*She hands her the note book.*] Well, we are glad you are not the spy.

ALOLIKA: What? Did you ever suspect *me*?

PARNAA: You insisted so much on keeping the note book! We all suspected you. You are lucky Pushpita made that call. Otherwise, we would have gagged you today and taken the note book from you.

ALOLIKA: I cannot believe you suspected me. Here, take the note book. I won't have anything to do with it! It's your headache now.

Parnaa takes the note book and again, brings it down on Alolika's head.

ALOLIKA: AAW!

PARNAA: I was pretending again! This was a back-up plan to see if you've learned your lesson. You have failed – again!

ALOLIKA: What? I...you! Stop it! Give me the note book! I've had enough of it.

Parnaa gives Alolika the note book. Enter Adrija from left.

ADRIJA: Hi!

ALOLIKA & PARNAA: Hi!

ADRIJA: [*To Parnaa*] Did you try it out?

PARNAA: Yes. [*Looks at Alolika.*] She failed both the times!

ADRIJA: Alolika! You have acted like yourself! You must be hard. Now give me the note book. I will show you how to keep it.

ALOLIKA: No, I won't!

ADRIJA: Give it to me!

ALOLIKA: No! Take it if you can.

PARNAA: Cool! You've finally succeeded.

ALOLIKA: [Jumping] Oh, good! I'm so glad. [*She keeps the note book inside her bag.*] You can't trick me again.

Enter Pushpita from left, wearing sunglasses.

PUSHPITA: Hello, dears.

PARNAA: She even dresses like a secret agent.

PUSHPITA: I'm sorry, I didn't get you.

ALOLIKA: Sweet words, hard nature. Lady Macbeth falls short before her.

ADRIJA: [*To Pushpita*] Hello! We are rather surprised to see you.

PARNAA:	[*Aside to Adrija*] Your words will arouse her suspicion!
PUSHPITA:	That's good. I want you to be surprised.
ALOLIKA:	Why do you want us to be surprised?
PUSHPITA:	Oh, no particular reason. I mean, I can't tell you now. It's a secret. If I tell you, it will ruin the surprise.
ALOLIKA:	And the secret.
ADRIJA:	And the agent.
PUSHPITA:	What?
ADRIJA:	Nothing.
PUSHPITA:	Did you find it?
ADRIJA:	No, I do not have it. You can search me if you want to.
PUSHPITA:	What?
ADRIJA:	[*Aware that her words were odd*] What?
PUSHPITA:	Why should I search you?
ADRIJA:	I don't know. You want me to search for the note book, so, you might feel like searching me for the note book, maybe.
PUSHPITA:	You are talking like crazy.

Her cell phone rings. She takes the call. She edges towards the left stage while she talks; the girls tiptoe behind her.

PUSHPITA:	Yes…No, I do not have it at the moment… [*The others exchange significant glances.*] …You'll get the matter in time, don't worry…Talk to you later. [*She ends the call,*

and turns around. The others turn back in a hurry and stop, then they slowly turn around to face her.]

You girls are not behaving properly today.

ALOLIKA: So, you will teach us how to behave?

PUSHPITA: Something is wrong with all of you. [*A pause*] Listen, I have to go now. Keep searching.

ALOLIKA: Won't you attend the classes?

PUSHPITA: No, I have important paper work to do.

Exit Pushpita from left.

PARNAA: What more proof do we need? Her words show that she is a spy. Her dress shows it, too. That sunglass!

ALOLIKA: We have to decipher the code. I was looking at it the other day, and some words come very close to English words.

PARNAA: That is a trick. We must read between the lines.

Alolika's cell phone rings. She takes the call.

ALOLIKA: Yes, we're here...downstairs? Great! We'll go down then. [*She ends the call.*] So, you guys must have heard it.

The other two look at Alolika apologetically.

Didn't you hear?

PARNAA:	Yes, we did. We know it's not polite to listen to other's conversation, but we could not help it.
ALOLIKA:	Well, it wasn't a private conversation, and I am not blaming you!
ADRIJA:	Well, then why did you ask us?
ALOLIKA:	So that I don't have to repeat it!
PARNAA:	Oh!
ALOLIKA:	Come on, let's go. The others were not willing to go up the stairs, so, they insisted on having the class downstairs. Archita – it was she who called – told that Sir has asked any one of us to bring the register. So, we'll have to take it to the class.

Exeunt from left. Lights fade out.

Scene II: College Corridor

Enter Sanhita from left and Pushpita from right.

SANHITA:	[*Very alert*] Oh, hello.
PUSHPITA:	Hello dear. I would have come near you, but I do not want to.
SANHITA:	So much the better.
PUSHPITA:	Please search for that note book. I need it by Wednesday.
SANHITA:	So, you give us two days' time.
PUSHPITA:	[*Assertively and enquiringly*] Yes. [*Normally*] Look, I have to go now. I have some work at hand. Talk to you later.

Exit Pushpita from left. Sanhita *quickly passes and leaves from right. She re-enters from right, followed by Ankit.*

ANKIT:	Hey, Sanhita!

Sanhita *keeps walking, as if she has not heard. Ankit runs and faces her.*

	Hi!
SANHITA:	Oh, it's you!
ANKIT:	How long do you think you can avoid me? Now give me the answer.
SANHITA:	Do you have to know?
ANKIT:	Yes!
SANHITA:	You want the truth?
ANKIT:	Yes!
SANHITA:	You can't handle the truth!
ANKIT:	Stop talking rubbish! I need the answer now.
SANHITA:	All right. [*Moves up stage, centre*] It was I who scribbled at the back of your shirt.[70]
ANKIT:	I knew it!
SANHITA:	But I never meant for you to find it out.
ANKIT:	Oh, you did it deliberately.
SANHITA:	Yes, but it was a one-time affair. It won't happen again.

---

[70] She had actually done written something at the back of his shirt.

ANKIT:	I do not want to talk to you right now. How could you do this to me?
SANHITA:	I am sorry. I will make sure you do not find it out the next time.
ANKIT:	What? The next time?
SANHITA:	Oh dear, what am I saying? I'll have to go now. I have a class to attend.

Exit Sanhita from right; Ankit shouts after her.

ANKIT:	I'll find out about the code language just as I have found out about you.

Exit Ankit from left. Lights fade out.

Scene III: The Arts Library – Reading Room

Barnali discovered sitting at table. Enter Alolika, Parnaa, Kankana and Adrija from right.

BARNALI:	Finally! I thought you'd not come.
KANKANA:	We are sorry. Ma'am kept on lecturing. It was overtime. She looked at her watch, and continued to speak. Finally, Prof. _____ called her to come to a meeting, and so, she ended the class.

They sit on chairs around the table. Alolika takes out the note book.

ALOLIKA:	Now let's see how much we can deduce.

They all bend their heads.

PARNAA:	I think this line means "Coming to your house".

KANKANA: No, it does not mean that.

PARNAA: [*Challengingly*] Oh! Have you any idea what it means?

KANKANA: Yes. I've systematically dis-arranged the alphabets.

ALOLIKA: Have you re-arranged them?

KANKANA: Yes. The line means, "Get the money ready".

ADRIJA: Barnali, please note these down! Why aren't you writing what we are saying?

BARNALI: Oh, so sorry. I was just thinking how much money she is making by doing this.

Everyone begins to ponder at this.

ALOLIKA: Ahem! We must get back to work.

They all bend their heads towards the note book. Lights dim out.

Act III

Scene I: College Portico

Enter Archita and Divya from left; Alolika and Parnaa from right.

ARCHITA: Hi! Any luck?

PARNAA: Yes. We have been able to decode the code.

DIVYA: Great! And it's Tuesday. We still have one day to plan how to capture her red-handed.

| ALOLIKA: | Yes. I do feel bad about her, but she has done this thing herself. |

Enter Barnali, Kankana and Adrija from right.

| BARNALI: | So, you must have heard it. |

| ARCHITA: | Yes. Congratulations. |

| BARNALI: | See you later. We're going to buy some books. |

Exeunt Barnali and Kankana from left.

| ADRIJA: | Give me that book for a few minutes, Alolika. I want to check something. |

| ALOLIKA: | [*Giving her the note book*] Here. |

Adrija takes it and smacks Alolika on the head.

| | AAW! It hurts! |

| ADRIJA: | Stop giving the note book, Alolika! Pushpita will be able to take it from you easily. It will be like offering candy to a kid! |

| ALOLIKA: | Kids do not take candy from strangers these days. |

| DIVYA: | Yes, they prefer money. |

| ALOLIKA: | Now give me that note book. |

She takes that note book. As she puts it inside her bag, Pushpita enters from left, wearing sunglasses.

| PUSHPITA: | Hello, dears. Have you found the note book? |

| ALOLIKA: | What makes you think we have? Did someone tell you? |

PUSHPITA: No, why will anyone tell me?

PARNAA: [*Aside to the others*] Look how she's not answering our queries, and evading *our* cross-questions with her own questions.

PUSHPITA: I require it by Wednesday. It would be better if I get it back today.

ALOLIKA: We really cannot help you.

PUSHPITA: But you must. You are my friends. [*She notices the cover of the note book.*] What is that bulging out of your bag, Alolika?

ALOLIKA: [*Zipping up her bag*] Nothing.

PUSHPITA: It is obviously something. It looked like my note book.

PARNAA: I'm sure there are several note books of the same design.

PUSHPITA: I dare say you are right. Still, why do you not want to show it to me?

ADRIJA: Why would we hide your note book? Stop accusing us.

PUSHPITA: I am not accusing you. What is the matter with you all?

ARCHITA: That is not your note book, Pushpita. That is Alolika's secret diary. She does not want us to see it. It has private matters.

PUSHPITA: Why did you bring it then?

ALOLIKA: Hey lady, stop being a detective! It depends on me how, where, when and why I bring my diary.

PUSHPITA: Are you trying to hide something?

ARCHITA: We were just going to buy some books. We're getting late. Come on. Let's go.

They all leave hurriedly from left. Pushpita stands staring at them.

PUSHPITA: Alolika never said anything about her personal diary before. I am sure it is my note book. But why are they hiding it from me? Maybe I am mistaken? [Pause] But I am sure they are hiding something. [Another pause] Anyway, let me search for it in the lounge. Maybe I left it there.

Exit Pushpita from right. Lights fade out.

Scene II: The Lounge

Ankit is seated on a sofa. The area is dark. Enter Pushpita from right, and switches on the lights. Ankit discovered.

PUSHPITA: Hi!

ANKIT: Hi! Please switch off the lights. I prefer sitting in the dark.

PUSHPITA: [*Beginning to search*] I prefer the light of knowledge.

ANKIT: That is very ironical, considering what you are doing.

PUSHPITA: [*Stopping and looking at him*] What?

ANKIT: I was merely speaking to myself.

Pushpita begins searching again.

PUSHPITA: It's not here. Well, Ankit, I have some work. I am leaving. Please tell if you find the note book.

Exit Pushpita from right.

ANKIT: She has ruined my mood. Let me go find the others.

Exit Ankit from right. Lights fade out.

Scene III: Outside College Gate

Barnali, Archita, Divya, Parnaa, Alolika and Adrija discovered outside the gate.

BARNALI: Well, that was a close escape.

PARNAA: She actually thought we went. Never bothered to check outside. Very careless of a secret agent!

DIVYA: So, what have you discovered? Tell us!

ADRIJA: Certainly not here. We can't reveal this in front of the others.

ARCHITA: That means the secret is really big! Too bad Sanjukta is out with her family. She could have helped in this.

DIVYA: Ankita would have definitely liked this.

ADRIJA: Why isn't she coming?

ARCHITA: She has plans with…you know who.

ADRIJA:	Ooohh!

BARNALI: Somebody's coming. [*She peeps in at the gate and withdraws at once*.] It's Pushpita. Quick. Let's disperse. We'll meet in Room No. 23 in five minutes.

PARNAA: Right. We'll go around and enter from the back-gate. Adrija, you go and stay in front of the stairs leading to Coffee House. Give us a missed call when she passes by. Barnali, you go towards CU and come back. Archita and Divya, you two go to a book store and come back.

They all disperse from left. Enter Pushpita from right.

PUSHPITA: Something is fishy. These girls are hiding something. Ankit is unusually queer today. I must find out what they are keeping back. Everyone seems to be avoiding me. Well, they should, as I have conjunctivitis. But they all seem so scared. I must spy on them and see what they are up to.

Exit Pushpita from left. Lights fade out.

Act IV

Scene I: Room no. 23

Enter Alolika, Parnaa, Archita, Divya, Kankana and Adrija from left.

ARCHITA: Tell us what you have found out.

DIVYA: No, wait a bit. Wait for the others.

Enter Barnali from left.

PARNAA: There you are! What took you so long?

BARNALI: I was talking with Professor CJA. He wants
                  to take an extra class to finish teaching
                  Dylan Thomas.[71]

ADRIJA: What did you say?

BARNALI: Well, as it is one class, I said yes. So, we
                  will have to come for the first period
                  tomorrow.

ADRIJA: But tomorrow is Wednesday. It's Operation
                  Lady Spy.

ARCHITA: Well, as it's the first class, it will be over by
                  10:50a.m. We can start our action then.

DIVYA: You have not even told us what you have
                  found out.

PARNAA: It was you who told us to wait for the others.

DIVYA: Yeah, right.

ALOLIKA: So, we've found out –

DIVYA: No, wait for the others!

ALOLIKA: Well, we do not know when they will turn
                  up – if at all they will turn up.

---

[71] This class actually took place. Prof. CJA went to the US for
some months, and before he left, he wanted to finish his
assignments. He asked the students to come for the first period on a
particular day, saying he would finish teaching a poem by Dylan
Thomas. This one period extended to over four periods, and this
historic epic class was held in the Professors' Common Room. The
poem had remained unfinished even after four classes.

DIVYA: I called them up when we were window-shopping some books.

PARNAA: Wow! You spent so much of your talk-time balance.

DIVYA: Desperate times call for desperate measures.

Enter Urbashi, Poulami, Sanhita, Bishakha, Sanchari and Indira from left.

BARNALI: How! Great job!

DIVYA: Thank you.

Enter Sara from left.

SARA: Wow! Almost everyone has gathered.

BARNALI: Can we please start now?

DIVYA: Of course! We must not wait for the other others.

Everyone sits on the benches. Barnali and the others who decoded the text go up to the table.

BARNALI: After careful observation, examination and correction and re-correction and revision and revision, this is what we have found out.

ALOLIKA: [*Beginning to read*] *Thursday, 10:00a.m.* [*To the others*] We couldn't decode the rest of the paragraph.

There is a groan.

ADRIJA: There is more. [*She begins to read. The others fall silent.*] *The tide. The army. Plunder. Laughter.*

PARNAA: *[Taking and reading the next part.]* It is Thursday. Do not be late. *[To the others]* We couldn't de-code ten lines after that.

The others groan.

KANKANA: But there is a bit more. *[Reading. The others fall silent.]* The Sun rises in the east.

BARNALI: Well, put together, this is what we have de-coded. *Thursday. 10:00a.m. The tide. The army. Plunder. Laughter. It is Thursday, do not be late. The Sun rises in the east.* We think she is going to start the action on Thursday at 10:00a.m. It will involve an army, who will reach their destination at the time when the tide comes up – 12 noon. They will plunder and laugh at their exploit. Then she sort of repeats her instructions. *The Sun rises in the east* might mean that the plunder will start somewhere in the eastern side, and so, *The Sun* is metaphoric for their victory.

POULAMI: Do you think she means our college?

BARNALI: That is extremely probable. We must prevent her.

BISHAKHA: We will tie her up and not let her go. So, the army will know something has gone wrong, and will not come.

INDIRA: We will also keep some policemen.

BARNALI: We must be together.

ALL: Yeah!

BARNALI:	Now we must tell the boys to help us.
ALOLIKA:	[*Lifting up the note book*] We will fight for ourselves!
ALL:	[*Getting up*] Yeah.
ALOLIKA:	We will bring down the traitor!
ALL:	Yeah!
ALOLIKA:	We are Presidencians!
ALL:	YEAH!!

Enter Pushpita from left.

PUSHPITA: My note book!

All heads turn. All bravery is forgotten. Everyone scampers to the back. Pushpita looks on. Lights dim out.

Scene II: College Gate

Enter Ankit from left.

ANKIT:	Finally! All the girls have disappeared!

Enter Harsh from left.

	Welcome buddy!
HARSH:	[*Taken aback*] *Welcome? Buddy?* Have you been drinking *bhang* again?
ANKIT:	No, but I will be, for I'm very happy!
HARSH:	You and your absurdity. Have you seen Bishakha? Is she – with the others – still on that crazy secret agent thing?
ANKIT:	She has disappeared!
HARSH:	WHAT??

ANKIT: So have all the other girls! It's our rule in the department.

HARSH: What??

ANKIT: Yes. Pushpita was the last to be seen. All the girls of the department! Disappeared! Now I can sit in darkness at the lounge.

HARSH: [*Aside*] He's crazy. I'll look around for Bishakha.

ANKIT: Where are you going? Let's celebrate! Come with me to the lounge. We'll call Saheb and Indra. No, wait, Indra is out of town. Anyway, we'll sit together in the darkness.

HARSH: Dude, you are mad. I'm not interested in such weird activities. I have to find Bishakha.

ANKIT: Hey, I'm in a good mood towards you now. Make the most of once in a blue moon.

HARSH: Look, I have to go.

Exit Harsh from left. There is a loud shout off-stage.

ANKIT: That sounds like the girls. It shouldn't be.

There is another cheer.

                Where are they? Are they invisible?

There is another cheer.

                How can they be invisible and beat the scientists? But then, there are many in the English Department who have come from

91

Science stream. We are privileged to have students from all the streams.

Enter Saheb from left. There are screams off-stage.

SAHEB: Where are the girls?

ANKIT: I was hoping they had disappeared. However, I have heard three shouts. They show distinct possibilities that they belong to the girls of our department.

SAHEB: Well, let's find them out. They are really being stupid about this spy thing.

ANKIT: *I* also believe that she is a spy. I do not like that she is doing it, of course. But I do like the fun we are having, except of course, when I am involved in it.

SAHEB: [*Peering over his glasses*] How have *you* been involved in it?

ANKIT: You are looking like our HOD.

SAHEB: I know. Now tell me.

ANKIT: I was hoping I would be able to change the topic by saying that.

SAHEB: Well, I am rather focused.

ANKIT: So I see.

SAHEB: Now please tell me how you have been involved with it.

ANKIT: I have talked with Pushpita.

SAHEB: Where? When?

ANKIT: Just a few minutes ago. I guess it will be ten minutes. I was sitting at the lounge. She told me she needs her note book, and then went out to do some "work". We all know what she means!

SAHEB: So you think.

ANKIT: And I am right. I am always right. [*A pause*] I think I am right. [*Another pause*] It's a possibility.

SAHEB: Yes, if you are talking about quantum dynamics.

ANKIT: *Et tu*, Saheb? [72] I thought you were in Humanities.

SAHEB: Yes, so?

ANKIT: But you are talking about quantum dynamics.

SAHEB: Yes, so?

ANKIT: Isn't that taught in Science?

SAHEB: Of course. When did I say it is taught in Humanities?

ANKIT: You were giving me that impression.

SAHEB: I never said that!

ANKIT: Yes, but you do know about it?

SAHEB: Yes, I do. So what?

ANKIT: [*Giving up*] Nothing.

---

[72] The allusion is to *Julius Caesar*. *Et tu* is Latin for "And you (too)".

SAHEB:	So shall we shop this discussion? We have to find the girls. You must engage them in conversation while I take the note book.

Ankit's cell phone rings. He takes the call.

ANKIT:	Yes, Sara…Where? Room no. 23? Oh!...What? You have caught Pushpita? Where?...Oh! Room no. 23…Yeah, that is great…You want us there?...OK, Saheb and I will be right there.

He ends the call.

	You will never guess what has happened.
SAHEB:	They have caught Pushpita in Room no. 23, and they are all there and they want us to be there.
ANKIT:	Yes! How did you know?
SAHEB:	You repeated everything she said.
ANKIT:	Oh!
SAHEB:	Now hurry up!

Exit Saheb from right.

ANKIT:	My bulging belly prevents me from going so fast. I'll just walk inside at a slow pace. After all, they have caught Pushpita. Now we'll have more fun.

Exit Ankit from right. Lights fade out.

Act V
Scene I: Room no. 23

Pushpita discovered tied up in a chair. Her sunglasses are dramatically still on.[73] All the girls surround her.

ALOLIKA: It was really brave of you to catch her from behind, Sanjukta.

URBASHI: Oh, I acted upon impulse. I was lucky she came so forward and I was behind her. Indira displayed exceptional common sense to go to the staff room and bring a coil of rope from Shyamal Da.

INDIRA: I acted upon visions.

BARNALI: Visions?

INDIRA: Visions from movies.

PUSHPITA: Let me go, you crazy people, and give me my note book.

ALOLIKA: Oh no, I have learned my lesson.

PUSHPITA: I will complain to the HOD and all the professors!

SANCHARI: What? Are they in this too? But this exceeds expectations.

PARNAA: Do not believe her. She is just trying to frighten us. I am sure the professors are not in this. Anyway, they are busy in a meeting.

SARA: Trying to frighten us? Pushpita, you will not have your wish fulfilled this time.

PUSHPITA: You are my closest friend over here! How can you do this to me?

---

[73] This is a mockery of the conventional image of the captured superhero, who somehow has his masks on all the time.

SARA: I, too, thought that you are my friend, and
                         was the last person to believe it. How could
                         you do this?

PUSHPITA: Do *what*?

ALOLIKA: Do not pretend innocent ignorance! We all
                         know you are an experienced secret agent.

PUSHPITA: Are you all out of your minds?

BARNALI: Listen, your pretence will not work with us.
                         We know vaguely what you are up to.

PUSHPITA: You have not even got the vaguest idea!

KANKANA: What? Is it more dangerous, then?

PUSHPITA: What are you talking about?

Enter Saheb from left.

SAHEB: What are you girls doing? You must be
                         crazy.

BARNALI: How can you not believe even when you see
                         the proof in front of your eyes?

BISHAKHA: Where's Harsh, by the way? His cell phone
                         is switched off.

SAHEB: I do not know where he is. Now let her go.

KANKANA: We will certainly not let her go.

The others nod in approval. Enter Ankit from left.

ANKIT: Wow! Cool capture!

PUSHPITA: Are you making alliterative jokes about me,
                         you bloody bourgeoisie?

KANKANA: She is working for the Russians or the Chinese!

BARNALI: Yes! That fits with "in the east" part!

PUSHPITA: Just shut your nonsense and let me go!

ANKIT: How did you capture her?

SARA: That is not the point now. Help us get her to speak out her secrets.

ANKIT: I will help you only if you update me as to how you captured her.

All girls groan and turn to Ankit. Saheb takes the opportunity and in a swift motion, snatches the note book from the desk where Alolika had accidentally placed it before turning to Ankit.

SAHEB: This is German!

KANKANA: [*Turning with the others*] What? She is working with the Germans?

PUSHPITA: No! I am learning German! That is my exercise copy. I need it for a test on Friday. I also need to give these notes to someone by tomorrow.

BARNALI: Nice try. But you will not fool us that easily.
SARA: Yeah. Your sunglasses are unmistakably the universal uniform of secret agents.
PUSHPITA: I have these on because I am suffering from conjunctivitis!

Everyone is silent for a few moments.

BARNALI: We need proof. [*To the others*] Somebody, please take off her sunglasses.

PARNAA: No one is willing to catch this infection.

97

SAHEB:	So, you believe she has conjunctivitis?
SARA:	That is a possibility.
ANKIT:	In quantum dynamics, right?
SAHEB:	Yes, if you are talking about parallel universe.
ANKIT:	What?
SAHEB:	I thought not. But let's not digress like our professors.

He goes and begins to untie Pushpita.

ALOLIKA:	What are you doing?
SAHEB:	Well, as no one, including me, is willing to take off her sunglasses, let her do it.
KANKANA:	What if she hasn't got conjunctivitis?
SAHEB:	Then we can tie her up again.
KANKANA:	Oh yeah! I forgot that.

Pushpita gets up and opens her sunglasses and glares at everyone. All the girls shut their eyes.

BARNALI:	Please put them back on! We have seen enough! We don't want to suffer from conjunctivitis! Why didn't you tell us before?
PUSHPITA:	You never gave me a chance.
SAHEB:	Here, take your note book.

Pushpita puts back her sunglasses and takes the note book.

ALOLIKA:	We're so sorry dear.

Pushpita hits her with the note book.

AAW! THAT HURTS!

PUSHPITA: Now I am having fun!

ALL THE OTHER GIRLS: We are really sorry. Please forgive us.

PUSHPITA: How can you possible think I was a spy?

ADRIJA: We tried to decipher the language. We thought it was a code language. We were wrong.

SARA: I wish I had looked at it.

BISHAKHA: Me too! I would have recognized the language at once!

PUSHPITA: [*Ignoring them*] But if you deciphered them, you will know there is nothing like the work of a secret agent. It's all filled with German greetings, sentences you would need to use in everyday conversation, and such types.

ALOLIKA: Well, we followed a methodical way.

PARNAA: We copied the alphabets of each paragraph separately, and then arranged them to form words.

KANKANA: And we formed only those words that would be used by a secret agent.

BARNALI: It did not fit all the time, but we were satisfied.

SAHEB: You all should teach the FBI.

URBASHI: Please do not be sarcastic now. [*To Pushpita*] Sorry I jumped on you.

ANKIT: [*Speaking resignedly*] Oh well, all the girls
                    are back. Not all of them – the ones who'd
                    disappeared. You know what I mean.

PUSHPITA: Thankfully, I don't.

ANKIT: I mean –

SARA: By the way, you said you were planning a
                    surprise for us.

PUSHPITA: Well, my birthday was last week, as you all
                    know.

Some girls slap their foreheads, then nod. Others look at others.

                    Well, I see not everyone knew, and the ones
                    who did know have forgotten.

POULAMI: We are so sorry!

PUSHPITA: I was planning to give you a treat. I am not
                    so sure about that now.

SARA: Have I said you look wonderful with those
                    sunglasses?

POULAMI: You are a very sweet friend, Pushpita.

KANKANA: You are extremely knowledgeable.

ADRIJA: Your watch is so good!

PUSHPITA: It will not work. I am not flattered.

All girls face away. Face down.

                    But I am touched at your closeness. I will
                    give you the treat after all.

ALL: Hurrah!

Enter Harsh from left.

BISHAKHA: Where have you been? Why is your phone switched off?

HARSH: [*Eyes only for Bishakha*] Switched off? I didn't know it was switched off.

BISHAKHA: Doesn't matter. Let's go outside.

Exeunt Harsh and Bishakha from left.

ANKIT: I am glad you all are reconciled.

PUSHPITA: So am I. now let's go out.

All begin to go out. They speak as they leave.

                    By the way, who found my note book?

PARNAA: I had sat upon it.

ALOLIKA: And I had opened it. So, we both found it.

PUSHPITA: So, you two started this thing?

ALOLIKA: [*Apologetically*] Yes.

PARNAA: The thing is, we were watching that film – Agent Cody Banks – it's about a teenage boy who is a secret agent. It's pretty cool. You should watch it.

Pushpita gives a murderous look.

ALOLIKA: I am afraid we were both still thinking about it when we found the note book.

They all leave. Lights fade out.

CURTAIN

IT

HAPPENS

ONLY WITH

PRESIDENCIANS[74]

(A COMEDY IN FIVE ACTS)

---

[74] The title of this play is an allusion to a Hindi film, *It Happens only in India.*

ACT I

SCENE I: The Professors' Common Room – Round Table

Barnali discovered sitting on a chair at the round table. Two other chairs are kept.

BARNALI: [*Looking at her watch*] When will she come? I hope I don't have to do the tutorial alone.

Enter Ankita from Left, panting

ANKITA: Sorry I am late.

BARNALI: You've finally come! What took you so long?

ANKITA: [*Taking a chair and sitting down*] Sorry to keep you waiting. I was delayed because...you know who...called me. I couldn't take it, as I did not hear it, as my cell phone was in the silent mode. I sent him an SMS.

BARNALI: You messaged him.

ANKITA: Yes, I sent him an SMS –

BARNALI: No, you do not *send* an SMS, you *message* somebody; [75] you do not *do* murder, you murder; you do not *do* singing, you sing; you do not *do* dancing, you dance.

ANKITA: Please! I accept that I was wrong. Don't go on with this. [*Barnali gives an amusingly*

---

[75] Now, the expression is to "text" somebody.

triumphant look] Wow! You do know a lot of grammar.

BARNALI: [*After a moment's reflection*] Yes, I do. But I did not know about this one. Saheb told me.

ANKITA: Oh!

BARNALI: Well, I'm glad he told me. Imagine our HOD correcting the mistake!

ANKITA: The thought is too revolting.

BARNALI: You have not yet explained what took you so long.

ANKITA: I told you – I was delayed in…messaging.

BARNALI: How can that delay you?

ANKITA: Well, I was walking down the road when he called. When I noticed that he'd called, I was standing in front of a Metro station.

BARNALI: I didn't know you take the Metro.

ANKITA: Normally, I don't. But there's such a congestion on the road today that I got down from the bus and took the Metro to reach on time.[76] I messaged him before entering the station, as our cell phones go out of network when we are underground. I missed the train

---

[76] This actually happened with Kankana. She, Barnali, Ankit and myself had planned to watch *Harry Potter and the Order of the Phoenix*. Kankana was the last person to arrive – fifteen minutes after the show had started – because she faced congestion on the road. She got out of the bus and took the metro.

	by one minute, which made me wait for nine minutes before the next train arrived.
BARNALI:	And that explains why I heard that extremely supercilious voice telling me, "The number you have dialed is not available".
ANKITA:	Yes.

[*A pause*]

	Well, she's late in coming.
BARNALI:	Well, as she enters the class suddenly after we have all settled, I expect she's doing the same here.
ANKITA:	Yeah. In a way, it's good – these tutorials, I mean. Especially as they are offered by the college totally free.[77]
BARNALI:	Yeah, but I wonder how good it'll be in the HOD's tutorial.[78]
ANKITA:	She'll teach us a lot of things.
BARNALI:	She'll expect we know them.
ANKITA:	That's the hope.
BARNALI:	No, it isn't.
ANKITA:	I was being ironical.

---

[77] In our college, in the Undergraduate departments, each student is assigned to a tutor (who is a professor of the department) to help him with his work. It's not tuition – this takes place in the college, and is simply giving extra care to the student's performance. This arrangement of providing tutorials started at Presidency in the like of the system which is there at Oxford. Of late, some other colleges have started giving "tutorials", following the system at Presidency.
[78] HOD means Head of the Department.

BARNALI: Oh! I have waited here for such a long time that I'm not that reflexive towards figures of speech.

ANKITA: [*Totally puzzled*] reflexive?

BARNALI: Yes. My metaphor was drawn from reflex action.[79] You see, when we touch something hot, we remove our hands. Our brain tells us to do so. Nerve cells pass through our brain from all parts of the body. When we touch a hot object, signals are sent to the brain. The brain receives these signals, and arranges them to send back the message "It's hot. Remove your hands". These nerve cells – neurons – tell us to do so, and we do it. Right now, my brain is not able to pick out your words and arrange them properly. The receptors to receive these signals are not working properly, as I am not that alert right now. So, I could not tell that you had uttered an irony.

ANKITA: I don't know what to say [*She looks around*]

             When will she come?

BARNALI: Why did she pick us?

ANKITA: I don't know.

A pause. Footsteps are heard

BARNALI: Do we hope or not hope that it is she?

---

[79] This sentence is an allusion to Oscar Wilde's *The Importance of Being Earnest*, where Dr. Chasuble states "My metaphor was drawn from bees" after stating to Miss Prism, "I would hang upon your lips".

ANKITA:	Let us put hopeful countenances on top of hearts and minds desirous to escape.[80]

Enter Shyamal Da from left

SHYAMAL DA:	Third years?
ANKITA:	Yes.
SHYAMAL DA:	Here for tutorials?
ANKITA:	Yes.
SHYAMAL DA:	She will not come. She is busy at the University.
BOTH:	[*In jubilation*] Yes!
BARNALI:	That means we can go [*They rise*].
SHYAMAL DA:	Wait. She told me to give this to you before she left [*Displays a sheet*].
BARNALI:	So why are you giving it to us after she has left?
SHYAMAL DA:	What? Are you pulling my leg?
BARNALI:	No! That is an indecent accusation![81]
ANKITA:	He used an idiom.
BARNALI:	Oh! [*To Shyamal Da*] I'm not very reflexive about idioms right now.
SHYAMAL DA:	Reflexive?

---

[80] The allusion is to *Macbeth*, where Lady Macbeth states that they must be like the innocent flower from the outside, but the serpent underneath. Here, Ankita talks about putting a hopeful countenance, when they are actually wishing that it is not her.
[81] Barnali takes it literally.

BARNALI: My metaphor was drawn from reflex action. When we…

ANKITA: Stop it. [*To Shyamal Da*] Please give it to us.

BARNALI: But she has left. He ought to have given it before she left. That is what he said she said.

ANKITA: He meant she told him – before she left, she told him – to give this to us.

BARNALI: Oh! [*To Shyamal Da*] We're sorry.

SHYAMAL DA: How dumb you girls are![82]

He hands Barnali the sheet. Exit Shyamal Da from left.

BARNALI: [*Reads*] "From your knowledge of Robert Browning's poetry (which you must have); from your awareness of the Victorian age and it's diction (as you must be aware of); from your comparative analysis of Browning's poetry with that of his wife (as you must have compared) and from your opinion of Browning's poems (as you must have formed), I want you to write a paper on Browning as a poet of the Victorian age, ushering or not, modern poetry. Submit it by Monday". [*Looks at Ankita*] Well, that is very simple.

ANKITA: You think so?

BARNALI: No, I was being ironical.

ANKITA: You said you are not reflexive about figures of speech.

---

[82] No anti-feminist remark is meant over here.

BARNALI:	The effect of the tranquiliser-sitting [83] for fifteen minutes is passing off. My senses are awake once more.
ANKITA:	But even at that time you had used a metaphor.
BARNALI:	Yes, I know. It is my habit to undermine myself.
ANKITA:	You mean you had been reflexive all this while?
BARNALI:	Of course. Now, let's go to the canteen.
ANKITA:	Let's go to the photocopying store now. I must get this photocopied. I cannot remember such a long assignment.

[*Exit Barnali and Ankita from left. Lights fade out.*]

SCENE II: College Campus.

Enter Sara from left. Her cell phone rings. She takes the call.

SARA:	*Hæñ, bol ré*…well, as no one has said we should not have the class, and as the class is in the routine, and as the Professor has also not said anything about not coming, and as there is no film-fest or seminar or agitation or declaration of results, we should have the class…why, downstairs…missed call? OK. I will give you a missed call when the Professor enters the classroom.

---

[83] That is, the sitting which has acted like a restoring agent, as a tranquiliser would do.

She hangs up and is about to exit from right. Enter Pushpita from left.

PUSHPITA: Hey, Sara.

SARA: [*Turning round*] Oh, it's you, Pushpita. Hi.

PUSHPITA: [*Walking up to her*] So, let's go to the canteen.

SARA: But we have a class now.

PUSHPITA: No, that class has been cancelled. Didn't you get the information?

SARA: No one told me.

PUSHPITA: Saheb messaged me. I told Ankit and told him to tell you as my talk-time balance was rather low. Didn't he tell you?

SARA: Ankit did call me up yesterday. He talked about, well, Nelson Mandela, George W. Bush, global warming, plastic pollution, JNU and Harry potter, but did not mention this!

PUSHPITA: Well, now you know it. So, let's go to the canteen.

SARA: Wait, I have to call Barnali and tell her that this class will not be held. [*She makes the call*] Yes, Barnali, listen…no, she will not take the class…well, as the next class is in the next period, and as the Professor has not said anything about not coming, and as we know the class is supposed to be held and as there is no event in the college at that time for the class to be dissolved, the next class will be held [*looks enquiringly at Pushpita, who nods*]...Well, we are going to the canteen.

Exit Sara and Pushpita from right. Enter Barnali from left.

BARNALI: [*Talking on the cell phone*] Where?...Oh, canteen? OK. I'll see you there. Bye...yes, I have reached college.

She ends the call.

This girl. She can never make anything short.[84] [*Looks at her watch*] Well, I am late, but as this class will not be held, I have half-an-hours before the next class. Well, let me go to the canteen.

Enter Kankana from left.

KANKANA: Hi! I've an hour's talk in store for you.

BARNALI: But I have only thirty minutes before the next class starts.

KANKANA: I was using a figure of speech – a hyperbole.

BARNALI: Oh, I'm not that reflexive about figures of speech right now.

KANKANA: Huh?

BARNALI: Yes, reflexive.

Kankana gives a puzzled look

Ankita will tell you. So, what is it that you want to say?

KANKANA: I was having a serious conversation with Saheb about my career.

---

[84] Sara actually has the habit of talking a lot over the phone.

BARNALI: Oh, I've had it too. What did he say to you?

KANKANA: Well, nothing definite. He told me not to worry now.

BARNALI: We all need to think about our careers.

KANKANA: I told him so. He told me to focus on doing what would enable me to get my career – studies or experience. He told me to keep my mind on studies – not do anything more than odd jobs – and after some educational qualification – minimum Bachelor's degree, which I'm doing now – I should send my resumé to some companies or post it on the internet. He said I need to be focused and do what I feel like doing, and stop thinking that I'm not good at something while I'm doing it. He told me to hone my skills.[85]

BARNALI: I'm sure there are many who will differ from his views.

Enter Saheb from left.

SAHEB: Hi!

KANKANA: We were just talking about you.

BARNALI: [*Suddenly remembering*] Oh, I told them I'd go to the canteen.

KANKANA: Did you tell them when?

BARNALI: [*Reflecting*] No.

---

[85] Kankana and Barnali have actually both had this type of conversation with me.

KANKANA: Then you can go later.

BARNALI: Yeah, you are right. Besides, I have to look up some books in the library.

SAHEB: How's your assignment shaping up?

BARNALI: I haven't started on it yet. I can gather material on all parts of the topic except the diction of poems of the Victorian age. Today is Thursday. We have to submit it by Monday.

SAHEB: You can read *English Versification Through the Ages*.[86]

BARNALI: That is great. Tell me – who's the author? What is the price?

SAHEB: The book is at present out of print.

BARNALI: Great! Then why did you mention it?

SAHEB: You can check in the library.

BARNALI: Oh, yeah! So, let's go.

SAHEB: I have to go to the library too. I have to take a book on linguistics.

KANKANA: I need to go to the library too. I have nothing else to do.

Exeunt Kankana, Saheb and Barnali from right. Lights fade out.

ACT II

Scene I: college Portico.

---

[86] There is no such book by this name, at least, not that I am aware of. This is an allusion to J.K. Rowling's *Quidditch Through the Ages*.

Enter Barnali and Ankita from right.

ANKITA: That was some tutorial.

BARNALI: I have it all inside my head.

ANKITA: Really?

BARNALI: Yeah. I have it all inside my head – muddled.

ANKITA: It's Friday. We meet gain her again on Monday – first period.

BARNALI: Have you prepared anything so far?

ANKITA: No! Why did she pick us?

She sits down.

BARNALI: I guess she wanted our development.

ANKITA: We're sure developing in some big way.

BARNALI: Do not speak ill of the elderly.

ANKITA: I didn't know you had such sentiments.

BARNALI: I don't. I merely meant that walls have ears.

ANKITA: You could have just said so.

BARNALI: [*Reflecting*] Oh, yeah.

ANKITA: Anyway, I'm in a soup. I haven't got anything prepared for the assignment. I have to abandon my plans of meeting with…you know who…to write the paper and submit it on Monday.

| BARNALI: | And I have to lessen my chatting. By the way, why am I standing here? Let me sit. We still have forty minutes before the next class. [*She sits.*] I want to show you this book that I borrowed from the library. [*She takes out a book.*] It's a good book. I have not read it, but it looks good. |

Ankita takes it and turns its pages.

ANKITA:	So, you are well into the assignment. I have prepared nothing.
BARNALI:	It won't take much time once you start on it.
ANKITA:	I do not know where to start.
BARNALI:	Just begin with Browning's birth, then go on to place him in the Victorian age, and show how well he fits into it. Then, in a new paragraph, use the information in this book to talk about the features of poetry that Browning uses. After that, in another paragraph, begin talking about his wife, then state how their poems are related and how they are different. Then, just give some concluding remarks.
ANKITA:	I thought you said you are muddled. But you have charted it out so systematically.
BARNALI:	Yes, I said that. Well, the fact that I said I'm muddled and then charted it out so systematically shows that I'm muddled.
ANKITA:	Yeah...whatever. I guess I will go to the photocopying store to photocopy this book.

Exit Ankita from left.

| BARNALI: | Let me go to the Girls' Common Room. |

Exit Barnali from right. Lights fade out.

Scene II: The Arts Library – Reading room.

Ankita discovered sitting on a chair in front of a table, with papers and books.

ANKITA: I will finish this paper today itself. The HOD will be very impressed. I will beat Barnali. All attention will be on me.

She writes for some time.

        But it's too *boring*. I'm so mad at her for coming up with such a holistic topic. We're students after all, not scholars. Perhaps I will feel better if I pour out my anger by writing a poem. Yes, I'll do that.

She takes up a paper, and begins writing. Lights dim out.

Scene III: The Professors' Common Room.

Enter Barnali and Ankita from left.

BARNALI: We must do it now. And she must not find it out.

ANKITA: Yeah, I can't believe how dumb I've been.

BARNALI: Let's just hope she does not find out that you have submitted pages full of abuse instead of the paper on Browning.

ANKITA: [*Opening one of the drawers*] I just wrote it for fun and then, instead of submitting the right one, I – by mistake – submitted the wrong one! No, it's not here.

She tries another drawer, and looks at Barnali.

I can't open it! It's locked.

BARNALI: Well, see if the key is somewhere.

ANKITA: Let's see.

She begins to search. A sound of footsteps is heard. Barnali goes to the left gate and comes back.

BARNALI: She's coming! We have to leave.

ANKITA: Not without my abuses!

Barnali pulls her from the table.

BARNALI: Come on. We have to leave now.

Exit Barnali and Ankita from right. The sound of footsteps becomes louder as the lights become dimmer. They fade out just as the person is about to enter.

ACT III

Scene I: College Portico

Enter Kankana and Sara from left, with bags over their shoulders.

KANKANA: We're before time. Let's sit down on the portico and talk for ten minutes.

They sit.

SARA: So, Barnali must have told you about Ankita's tutorial disaster.

KANKANA: Yes. She had to force Ankita out of the staff room. Imagine her entering and catching them going through her property.

SARA: They are at their tutorial now, aren't they?

KANKANA: Yes. I'm lucky I don't have a tutorial in the first period. Poor Barnali and Ankita. HOD's tutorial. That too, *our* HOD.

SARA: Has Ankita come?

KANKANA: She was supposed to. Both of them were supposed to submit their assignments today. It was really stupid of Ankita to write such stuff and confuse it for the actual assignment.

SARA: Ankita told me last night that she was chatting on the cell phone with her...you know who...when she mixed up the papers. Now, the warning signs should read "Do not talk or message on the cell phone while driving, crossing roads or submitting assignments".

They laugh. Enter Ankit from left.

ANKIT: Hi! Aren't you attending class?

SARA: Aren't you?

ANKIT: But the class is supposed to start after five minutes.

The two girls look mockingly pitiful.

             Oh, right! I've got it.

KANKANA: It's a surprise that you have come so early.

ANKIT:	I couldn't resist the temptation of eating such a wonderfully spicy news.
SARA:	Don't you feel sorry for her?
ANKIT:	Of course I do. But the matter is so humorous. I wanted to relish every bite of it, so I came early.
SARA:	Talking of humour – are you still under the effects of *bhang*?
ANKIT:	Kindly do not bring up that subject. It was stupid of me to have drunk *bhang* and laugh all the time yesterday.[87] [Aside] I have drunk a little *bhang* today also, but they won't find it out. Hee, hee.

Enter Barnali with a wild Ankita.

BARNALI:	Hi!
SARA:	Hi! What happened?
BARNALI:	Well, she came with the abusive papers folded in her hands.
SARA:	Papers? How much abuse did you write?
ANKIT:	Hee, hee hee, hee hee.
ANKITA:	You think it's funny, do you?
ANKIT:	Of course! Hee, hee.
KANKANA:	Have you been drinking *bhang* again?
ANKIT:	How did you know? You must be a detective.

---

[87] Ankit actually drank *bhang* during his first year in college, and a few other times.

BARNALI:	You should sympathise.
ANKIT:	Believe me, I have lots of sympathy. I'll try not to laugh.
BARNALI:	As I was saying, she had just taken it out of the drawer, and had not looked at it. She looked at it after she sat down. You should have seen her face!

Ankit covers his mouth with his hands.

ANKITA:	[*Shakily*] She asked, "What is the meaning of this? Who wrote this?" Barnali produced her assignment and said, "Mine is here".
BARNALI:	Ankita took out her assignment and said, "So is mine". So, she thought someone else had written that.
ANKIT:	So she let you off? Great! Now I can laugh.
RBARNALI:	Yes and no.
KANKANA:	What do you mean?
BARNALI:	Let me quote her. She said, "This is a government college. Everything has to be done in a systematic way."[88]
ANKITA:	[*Passionately*] She has decided to set up an investigation committee.[89]

---

[88] She did actually say so on one occasion, though that had nothing to do with such an occasion.

[89] Once, we had decided to take out a departmental magazine. It was all running smoothly, till it was thought that there must be a committee to look into the formation of the departmental

Ankit bursts into laughter.

KANKANA: What?

BARNALI: Yes. I'll tell you about it after this class. Let's go.

Exit all the girls from right, Ankit following, laughing. Lights fade out.

Scene II: College Campus

Enter Indira and Sanchari from right.

INDIRA: That is some news Barnali gave us.

SANCHARI: Yes. Now hurry up. Let's go and buy those books.

Exit Sanchari and Indira from left. Enter a reporter and a photographer.

REPORTER: Remember to get a good view of it[90].

PHOTOGRAPHER: There's nothing wrong with my photography. It's only your reports that are rubbish.

REPORTER: What did you say?

PHOTOGRAPHER: Nothing. We have to hurry. I have to go to four other colleges.

---

magazine. As this was not at all a practical idea, the departmental magazine was never produced.

[90] Reporters and photographers regularly throng our college campus.

REPORTER: We will go there from here. But mind, you are working under me, so you'd do well not to anger me.

PHOTOGRAPHER: I will keep that in mind.

REPORTER: Anyway, you never told me why the editor told us to go to four other colleges. In fact, I'm surprised that he told *you* and not me.

PHOTOGRAPHER: You had gone for having your lunch. He came in and told me.

REPORTER: What did he tell you?[91]

PHOTOGRAPHER: Well, two bombs have been blasted in A_____ College; classes have been abandoned in B_____ College; a professor has allegedly misbehaved with a girl in C_____ College and the Principal of D_____ College has been caught taking bribe to admit a student who does not qualify.

REPORTER: All minor incidents! Nothing compared to the mal-functioning door. This must make headlines. After all, it's Presidency.[92]

PHOTOGRAPHER: Will the readers be interested in reading it?

REPORTER: Do you think we'll report as things are? Of course not! The headline will run, "Excessive Grant Falls Short to Maintain

---

[91] This is merely being said in this way for the knowledge of the audience.

[92] This need not be the view of all reporters, but of this fictitious character. I am not aware of any such incident about a reporter desirous for a cover story on this or such issues.

Infrastructure". The report will focus on the fact that the maintenance of the rooms is very poor. The picture of the damaged door will suffice. And to speak the truth, not many will read the story. But everyone will look at the heading. The impression will be that the government is not doing enough for Presidency.

PHOTOGRAPHER: Even then, this college is far better in its classrooms.

REPORTER: Yes, but we do not care, do we? We just need a good story.

PHOTOGRAPHER: Even then, I feel we should write about something else.

Re-enter Indira and Sanchari from left.

INDIRA: This is the most interesting thing that has ever happened in our college.

SYTAPA: Yeah.

Enter Shyamal Da from right.

SHYAMAL DA: Third years?

STTAPA: Yeah.

Shyamal Da hands them a leaflet each. Exit Shyamal Da from right.

SANCHARI: [*Reading*] I, the HOD of the English Department, hereby invest Harsh Chakraborti, 3rd year, with the power to investigate into the matter of the scandalous papers to find the accused, who will stand for trial. Indra Roy, 3rd year, is hereby appointed as the Lawyer for Prosecution.[93] If found guilty, the accused shall face severe consequences, including the receipt of a notorious character certificate".[94]

INDIRA: Harsh as the detective!

SANCHARI: Indra as a lawyer!

INDIRA: Poor Ankita. I hope Harsh does not catch her.

Exit Indira and Sanchari from right.

REPORTER: Forget the door. I've got a new story.

Exit Reporter and Photographer from right. Lights fade out.

Scene III: The Arts Library – Reading Room

Enter Harsh from right with a magnifying glass in one hand, and an ink pad and some rolled-up sheets in the other. He sits down on one chair and spreads the papers.

Enter Barnali from right.

BARNALI: So, where do I have to give my fingerprints?

HARSH: [*Pointing at a paper*] Right here.

Barnali does so. Harsh writes her name underneath the fingerprint. Exit Barnali from right. Enter Indira from right.

INDIRA: [*In mock curiosity*] How's your work going?

---

[93] It is of course not possible for an HOD to invest such powers in reality.
[94] This trial-body is the influence of the story *Eric, or, Little by Little*.

HARSH:	[*Gruffly*] Fine. Just give me your finger-prints.

Enter Sanchari from right, followed by Sara, Ankita, Kankana, Pushpita and a scowling Ankit.

INDIRA:	Hi guys! Did you hear what he did?
HARSH:	Just shut up.
ANKIT:	What did he do?
INDIRA:	He went to the HOD to get her fingerprints. I was there for my tutorials with S_____ Sir, and we saw it.

There is a peal of laughter.

HARSH:	In my defense, I was just trying to make sure that I know her fingerprint, so that I don't put it as belonging to an imposter.
INDIRA:	But she thought you were trying to label her as a possible suspect. She slapped you!
HARSH:	Just give your fingerprints and clear out!
ANKIT:	[*Taking a step forward*] Hold on. This is not your home. You can't order us out.
HARSH:	Very well. Stay if you want to.

Ankit sits down.

SARA:	Come on Ankit, you don't want to sit here.
ANKIT:	I will sit here.

His cell phone rings. He takes the call.

	Oh, it's you…Where?...OK…Yes, I'll be there in a minute. [*He ends the call*.] That was one of my friends.

KANKANA: [*Sarcastically*] Oh, we thought it was your enemy.

ANKIT: No, that was one of my friends. I have to go see him in College Square.

He gives his fingerprints. Exit Ankit from right.

INDIRA: Well, Harsh, here you go. I am a possible suspect. But I will slap you if you accuse me.

There is a peal of laughter. Indira gives her fingerprints and so do the others. Exit all girls from right. Lights fade out on Harsh as he is trying to examine them in detail.

Scene IV: College Campus.

Enter Harsh from right and Barnali and Kankana from left.

HARSH: There you are. I want all of you in the playground. Tell the others.

BARNALI: Has everybody given the fingerprints?

HARSH: Yes.

BARNALI: Have you found out the culprit?

HARSH: I'll tell you when you all assemble in the play-ground.

Exit Harsh from left.

KANKANA: It's Tuesday. He did it in just one day! That is a great achievement.

| BARNALI: | Let's go find Ankita. I hope Harsh hasn't found her out to be the culprit. |

Exit Barnali and Kankana from right. Lights fade out.

Act IV

Scene I: Room No. 23

The big table for the professor stands at right stage, back corner, at an angle facing left stage, front corner. There are four chairs on the left of the table, facing the audience. A big chair is at the back of the table. At right corner, front stage, a bench is kept. Another such bench is kept at the back stage, centre, after the four chairs. The rest of the back stage, centre, and left stage are lined with benches. Two more chairs are kept in front of the four chairs, at such angles so as not to obstruct the four chairs.

Enter Sanjukta and Indra separately from left and place themselves on the two benches on two sides of the table.

INDRA:	You must know that I'm prosecuting Ankita.
SANJUKTA:	You must know that I'm defending Ankita.
INDRA:	You might as well give up the case. [*Rises.*]
SANJUKTA:	You might as well give up the case. [*Rises.*]
INDRA:	I know that basically, Ankita came to you after Harsh caught her.

SANJUKTA: Isn't that obvious?

| INDRA: | Basically, my gentlemanly nature *per se* keeps me from hitting you. |

SANJUKTA: My dignity of womanhood keeps me from lashing out at you.

INDRA: Unmannered shrew![95]

SANJUKTA: Fat Bumble![96]

INDRA: Girls!

SANJUKTA: Boys!

They seat themselves without any more word. Both avoid looking at each other. Enter Archita, Parnaa, Divya, Alolika, Pushpita, Indira, Sanchari, Poulami and Ankit from left and seat themselves on the benches lined for them. Enter Sara with a laptop, and sits beside Sanjukta. Enter Katha with a sheaf of papers and sits beside Indra.

Enter Shobha, Harsh, Maya and Panchali from left, bringing in a tearful Ankita.

SHOBHA: I am so sorry, Ankita. Apparently, the HOD thought I am strong enough to serve as a police-woman.

PANCHALI: Me too.

MAYA: At least you get to sit. We have to stand and keep guard and see that you do not escape.

HARSH: I'm privileged to get special treatment. As the detective, I get to sit up close and personal, ha, ha. [*Nobody laughs.*] It was a joke. [*No laughter.*] I have to go sit down. [*He takes a seat.*]

---

[95] The allusion is to *The Taming of the Shrew*.
[96] The allusion is to Charles Dickens' *Oliver Twist*, where Mr Bumble is a fat character.

Enter the Reporter and the Photographer. Everyone stares at them.

REPORTER: Nothing to turn your heads for. Your HOD
                   has given me permission to stay and report,
                   provided I do not speak. [*He shows a paper.*]
                   Your Principal had some objections, but
                   your HOD is really some lady! The Principal
                   let her have her way.

*They go and stand at the corner. Enter Ananya, Sreetama, Devi
and Kankana and take the four chairs. They are the jury. Enter
Shyamal Da from left.*

SHYAMAL DA: Third years?

SANJUKTA: [*Exasperated*] You *know* we are third years.

SHYAMAL DA: Hey, don't you give me any cheek, missy.
                   Listen, the HOD will not be able to come.
                   She is busy at the University.

ANKITA: [*Rising rapidly*] That means we are
                   dismissed?

SHYAMAL DA: No, she has appointed S_____ Sir as
                   the presiding chief.

Exit Shyamal Da from left. Enter Saheb and Barnali from left.

SAHEB: Listen everyone. You know S_____ Sir
                   was supposed to preside over this trial.
                   However, he does not wish to do so.

BARNALI: So, he, as usual, told me to do it. I, as usual,
                   told Saheb, Saheb has spoken to
                   S_____ Sir and the HOD and they
                   have agreed that he is going to be the
                   Presiding Chief.

Barnali takes a seat among the other students.

SAHEB: [*To the Reporter.*] What are you doing here?

REPORTER: We have permission. [*He flips the paper at Saheb.*]

SAHEB: Well, you can stay here, but you'll have to hand over the camera.

PHOTOGRAPHER: What?

SAHEB: It says that you can report. Nowhere is it written that you can take pictures.

PHOTOGRAPHER: I'm not giving the camera.

REPORTER: [*Taking the camera*] Oh, give it. The report is what matters. *He gives the camera.*

Saheb goes up to the big table and sits behind it, placing the camera on the table.

KATHA: [*Rising and coming forward*] Ladies and gentlemen, members of the jury, lawyers and the PC – we have gathered here today to witness a historic trial. Ankita, the accused, stands trial for allegedly writing insolent words to the HOD.

INDRA: Thank you, Katha, I'll take it up from here.

He stands; Katha sits. Sara is typing all the words and actions. She is the recorder of this proceeding.

Basically, Ankita has written some indecent lines about the respected HOD and must suffer the penalty.

SAHEB: I understand, Ankita, that you have selected Sanjukta as your lawyer?

ANKITA: Yes.

SAHEB: Sanjukta, how do you plead?

SANJUKTA: Not guilty.

SAHEB: Very well, Indra, you may proceed.

INDRA: Basically, I have nothing more to say, for the moment.

SAHEB: Don't you want to call anybody?

INDRA: Oh, yes, of course. But I wish to speak to the accused first.

SAHEB: You are permitted to do so.

INDRA: Ankita, do you confess to having written those lines?

ANKITA: I cannot answer you till you specify which lines you mean.

INDRA: I mean those lines which you spitefully wrote to insult her. I mean those lines which you dared to submit instead of the assignment. I mean those lines which you wrote in papers where your fingerprints have been identified. I mean those lines which have been brought to the trial to bear evidence against you.[97]

SAHEB: Katha, give me a copy of these papers. Indra, please read out the lines so that everyone knows what is there. [*There is a murmur among the students.*] And by the way, Indra, that was an excellent epanaphora.

INDRA: I beg your pardon?

---

[97] These lines are structured in the way Edmund Burke delivered his lines in his speech on *The Impeachment of Warren Hastings*.

PRESSY DAYS | NILANKO MALLIK

SAHEB: It's also called anaphora. Please continue with the proceedings.

INDRA: Yes, of course. [*Aside*] So, Edmund Burke used anaphora in his speech on *The Impeachment of Warren Hastings*. I have studied that speech, but I did not know this term.

KATHA: [To Indra] Won't you take this? Or have you memorized it? [*There is a peal of laughter.*]

INDRA: Yes, of course. I'll take it.

Katha gives him one copy, and one to Saheb. Indra reads in a dramatic fashion.

"*To, the Professor who is a necessary tolerable body,*[98] *I dedicate this poem.*

The sky is clear, the sun shines bright,
Students in canteen laugh with all might,
The heart and mind counsel to break,
Away from studies, down the steps take
Their ecstasy. But that dear she,
The indispensable, impossible she,[99]
Forces us down to scholarly assignment
Forcing to stay hours in bookish
confinement.
So I write this for my anger's catharsis,[100]

---

[98] The comparison is with the state as a necessary evil.
[99] The allusion is to a poem.
[100] This is an allusion to Aristotle's *Poetics*, where Aristotle mentions catharsis to be the prime motive behind watching tragedy. The nearest English translation of this word is, till date, purgation.

And hope she stays away like Homer's
Ulysses,[101]
So I don't feel like spurning her currish
work,[102]
But punch it hard and shout "You suck!"
My pen may break, and papers fly,
But this poem in reader's memory will
imprinted lie.[103]
That is not all. I also feel like saying that she
is so regular in making us feel wicked that I
wonder how she tolerates herself!"

[*He looks up*] Well, the malicious intention of the person is quite clear. I think we all feel that the hatred that is roused inside us for the composer – who is sitting right here – will frame our judgement to bring out the extremely affable nature of the professor.

Some students applaud. Indra sits down.

SAHEB: Sanjukta, have you anything to say?

SANJUKTA: Yes, I do. [*She rises.*] I think we are quite clearly not focusing on the right part. The lines of the poem [*She walks toward Indra and snatches the papers from him*] read "Away from studies, down the steps take/Their ecstasy". It should have been "The heart and mind counsel to break/Away from studies *and* down the steps take/Their ecstasy". Why is the *and* missing? This clearly shows the poet is not sure of the

---

[101] Homer's Ulysses spends a long time travelling, before finally reaching his place.
[102] The allusion is to *Julius Caesar*, where Caesar, just before his assassination, states, "I spurn thee like a cur out of my way".
[103] The closing couplet is in the shape of Shakespeare's couplets in his sonnets.

matter. Or that there are some other interpretations which we are missing out.[104]

There is general laughter.

SAHEB: Do you even have a point?

SANJUKTA: No, but that is what we must find out.

ANKITA: I thought you were defending me!

SANJUKTA: I am.

SAHEB: Please proceed.

SANJUKTA: Thank you. As I was saying, the missing *and* shows that the composer was not sure of the matter. As such, no offence should be taken from it.

INDRA: You are clearly after a wild goose chase.

SANJUKTA: Since when have you been hitting the bull's eye with your usual *pot pourri* [105] of irrelevant questions in almost every class? [*There is a general laughter. The jury nods.*] As I have pointed out, no offence should be taken for words which come out of confusion.

---

[104] Sanjukta actually said something similar in a class in our third year. While studying Browning with the HOD, she voiced her view that the lover says "One *more* last ride together" in *The Last Ride Together*. It should be either "One last ride together" or "Or more ride together", and thereby, gave a new interpretation regarding the narrator's motive, which was unique, but the interpretation being unconventional, suffered rejection.
[105] Pot-full.

INDRA:	There are other lines in the poem. Surely the jury will realize the deliberate malice in them? [*The jury nods.*]
SANJUKTA:	Surely the jury will accept that if *part* of the poem can come out of confusion on part of the poet, there's no guarantee that the *rest* is free of confusion? In fact, the odds are against it. [*The jury nods.*] That's all I have to say to you now. [*She sits.*]
INDRA:	[*Rising*] I would like to call my first witness, Mr Harsh Chakraborti.
SAHEB:	Permission given.
KATHA:	Harsh Chakraborty, please come to the witness stand.
HARSH:	[*Approaching*] You mean this chair?

Sanjukta snorts. Harsh glares at her, then sits.

KATHA:	[*Bringing The Concise Oxford Dictionary*] Please repeat. I give my word…
HARSH:	I give my word…
KATHA:	That whatever I say…
HARSH:	That whatever I say…
KATHA:	Here as a witness…
HARSH:	Here as a witness…
KATHA:	Is accurate in meaning, as per the entries in this dictionary.
HARSH:	Is accurate in meaning, as per the entries in this dictionary.

Katha goes and sits. Indra comes forward to question him.

INDRA: So, Mr Harsh –

SAHEB: Mr Chakraborty or Mr Harsh Chakraborty. You must speak the full name or the surname after 'Mister' or 'Mrs', and not just the name.

INDRA: I am sorry. So, Mr Chakraborty, is it true that you took the fingerprints of *all* the students of third year, including yourself?

HARSH: Yes, I did.

INDRA: And you also checked the fingerprints that are in the abusive papers?

HARSH: Yes.

INDRA: Did anyone's fingerprints match?

HARSH: Yes.

INDRA: Please tell us the name of the person.

HARSH: Ankita Sarkar.

INDRA: Thank you. This clearly proves that Ankita is the culprit. [*He sits.*]

SANJUKTA: [*Rising*] I would like to question him.

SAHEB: Please do.

SANJUKTA: [*Coming forward to Harsh*] Harsh, how many hours did you take to study the fingerprints?

HARSH: [*Proudly*] Sixteen hours.

SANJUKTA: Did you pause in your work?

HARSH:	[*Proudly*] No, I did not.
SANJUKTA:	Point to be noted. [*Sara nods.*] Harsh, is it not true that you have kissed Ankit several times?

Everybody laughs, except Ankit, Indra, Harsh and Sanjukta.

INDRA:	Objection. This has no relevance to the case.
SAHEB:	Objection overruled. This is extremely interesting.
SANJUKTA:	Thank you. Please answer the question.
HARSH:	[*Quietly*] Yes, I did.
SANJUKTA:	So, were these in front of others, or in secret?
HARSH:	[*Protesting*] No, not in secret. They were in the open. [*Several girls murmur.*] There were several girls present on all those occasions. [*Some girls nod.*]
PGOTOGRAPHER:	[*To the reporter*] I'm glad I don't have my camera. I would have surely dropped it.
SANJUKTA: Are you gay, Harsh?	
HARSH:	Of course not. I have a girlfriend. [*He looks at the others.*] She is not here at the moment, thankfully.
SANJUKTA:	So, you confess that you have engaged yourself in activities which are not considered appropriate for someone who is straight?
HARSH:	[*Hesitatingly*] I dare say I have. [*Vehemently*] But so what? Everyone

engages in this and that activities. I am not a saint.

SAHEB: Is this your idea of litotes? I'm not framing a rhetoric question.

HARSH: Huh? I didn't get you.

SAHEB: Your litotes will have a bad mark on you.

HARSH: So what? As I said, I am not a saint.

SANJUKTA: What do you mean? Please specify. What do you do?

HARSH: Well, I do not mean that I steal, but I lie, I have also fought some guys. I can be pretty rude, and I also abuse.

There is a general murmur at this word.

SANJUKTA: Point to be noted. [*Sara nods.*] So, you abuse. Might I bring to your recollection that the papers are allegedly *abusive*?

HARSH: I am quite aware of that.

SANJUKTA: Do you write similar abuses?

INDRA: Objection.

SAHEB: Objection overruled.

SANJUKTA: Thank you. So, could you have written similar abuses?

HARSH: I wish to maintain my right to remain silent.

SANJUKTA: That has put you in a grave realm of suspicion.

The jury nods.

HARSH: Please. I need a cigarette. I need to think properly.

SANJUKTA: [*Paying no attention*] You checked the fingerprints, did you not?

HARSH: [*Gruffly*] I have already answered in the affirmative.

SANJUKTA: Would you affirm to re-checking of the fingerprints?

HARSH: No, I did not re-check them.

SANJUKTA: Point to be noted. You abuse, and wish to remain secretive on whether or not you could have written similar abuses. You worked without pause for sixteen hours. You were definitely stressed. You may have made a mistake. However, you have not re-checked the fingerprints. We cannot take your verification, for they have not been verified.

HARSH: [*Pleading*] I will re-check them if you like, but I need a cigarette.

SANJUKTA: Why can't you do it before having a cigarette?

HARSH: I am so muddled right now.

The others murmur at this word.

SANJUKTA: Point to be noted. We have already noted that the poet was in a confused state while writing the poem. The similarity must be noted. [*The jury nods.*] Suspicion hangs on you, Harsh. That is all I have to say to you now. [*She sits.*]

KATHA: Harsh, please go back to your place.

Harsh goes and sits; Indra stands.

INDRA: I would now like to bring my second witness, Barnali Das.

SAHEB: Permitted.

KATHA: Barnali Das, please come to the witness chair.

Barnali comes and sits on the witness chair. Katha comes with the Dictionary, and Barnali gives her word.

INDRA: So, Miss...Barnali Das, when did you first hear the words of the abusive papers?

BARNALI: Today, in this room, when it was read out.

INDRA: You knew nothing about it before?

BARNALI: Of course I knew. That's why I came to the trial. Everyone knows. Do you think they gave their fingerprints for fun?

INDRA: How dare you answer me like that? How could you have the courage to talk to me like that?

SAHEB: She has used an excellent figure of speech – a rhetorical question, filled with sarcasm. She must be applauded for the use of this figure of speech, as we are students of literature, and must not be discouraged or scolded. However, I must tell you all not to bring personal issues in this trial. Please continue.

INDRA: Ahem! So, did you read this before?

BARNALI:	No, I did not. I already said that.
INDRA:	You were seen going with Ankita inside the staff room at a time when no professor was there – on Friday.
BARNALI:	Yes, we did. To submit the assignment.
INDRA:	But I was under the impression that you submitted the assignment on Monday.
BARNALI:	Yes. We had gone inside to submit Ankita's assignment.
INDRA:	[*Like Sherlock Holmes*] Aha!
BARNALI:	But she could not submit her assignment, as the drawer was locked, and we couldn't just leave it on the desk.
INDRA:	Why would anyone try to submit anything before time? That is very suspicious. [*The jury nods.*] Thank you, Miss Barnali Das.

He sits down.

SAHEB:	Sanjukta, would you like to question her?
SANJUKTA:	Yes. [*She rises.*] Miss Barnali Das, you say that the drawer was locked when you went to submit your assignment.
BARNALI:	Ankita's assignment. She wrote it in college after I gave her an outline of the answer, and we went together to submit it. It is acknowledged by all students of the department that nobody likes to face our HOD all by himself or herself.
SANJUKTA:	Yes, of course. [*She turns to the jury.*] I must ask the jury to reason out by common sense that if the drawer was locked, Ankita could

not have placed the abusive papers inside it. [*The jury nods.*]

Did you, Miss Barnali Das, go to the staff room that day before it was locked?

BARNALI: 'It'? Do you mean the staff room or the drawer?

There is general laughter.

SANJUKTA: [*Impatiently*] Please apply your common sense. Obviously, I mean the drawer.

BARNALI: Well, in a trial, you must be on your guard. [*The jury nods.*] To answer your question, I have to say that no, I did not enter it – the staff room, that is – that day at any other time.

SANJUKTA: [*Turning to the audience*] Everyone knows that it was kept on that day, that is, Friday, otherwise the HOD would have noticed it on Friday morning and not on Monday morning. Thank you, Barnali.

KATHA: You may go back to your seat, Barnali.

Barnali goes back.

SANJUKTA: It has been proved that the composer was confused; that Ankita and Barnali went in together and found the drawer locked. The abusive papers were clearly submitted at another time. There is a similarity between the confused state of the composer and that of Harsh Chakraborty. He has confessed that he abuses.

INDRA: [*Rising*] Harsh has not confessed to writing *those* abusive lines. He has maintained his right to remain silent.

SANJUKTA: Then that is more suspicious. What is he afraid of revealing? [*The jury inclines forward.*] There is strong suspicion in that attitude.

INDRA: The fingerprints do not match with him, but with Ankita.

SANJUKTA: They were checked by Harsh. Has anyone else confirmed it? No one has.

INDRA: No one has seen him go inside the staff room that day.

SANJUKTA: That is very unfortunate for us, that he was not seen. But it does not rule out the possibility that he *might* have gone there. After all, we have strong grounds to suspect him. [*The jury nods.*]

HARSH: I need a cigarette.

SANJUKTA: [*Paying no attention*] I have stated what I had to state. It is now for the jury to decide on the case.

The jury sits alert.

SAHEB: Indra and Sanjukta, please take your seats. [*They sit.*] I ask the jury to go inside the computer room to decide on the issue, and come to present their decision in written statement, in half an hour.

The jury files out from left.

SAHEB: The trial will resume after half an hour.

Exit Saheb from left, with the camera.

KATHA: The court will meet after half an hour.

Everyone begins to go out from left. Lights fade out.

Scene II: The Computer Room of the English Department.

Enter Devi, Ananya, Sreetama and Kankana from left.

DEVI: [*Looking around*] Wow. This is the first time
                     I have been in here.

KANKANA: You hardly come to college.

SUHESHNA: [*To Sreetama*] So, what do you think?

SREETAMA: I think Ankita wrote it.

KANKANA: I *know* Ankita wrote it.

DEVI: Really?

ANANYA: But how did you know?

KANKANA: She told it to Barnali, and Barnali told it to
                     me. Obviously, she did not know – neither
                     did I – at that time that the HOD was going
                     to choose me as a member of the jury.

SREETAMA: So, what should we do?

KANKANA: We know Ankita has done it. But can she be
                     blamed for it? I mean, is she really guilty?

ANANYA: I guess not, but then, she should not have
                     written such stuff. That was not morally
                     right.

145

SREETAMA: We are not here to judge morally.

KANKANA: Yes. That is up to God. The most that we can do is keep doing what our conscience tells us is right.

ANANYA: Conscience tells us that what she did was wrong.

DEVI: It was to herself that she wrote. She had never meant them to be known, though I guess she had written them with much bitterness.

SREETAMA: Well, we are all bitter with some things or somebody. And we need to speak out what we feel. She did just that.

KANKANA: Yes, it was like pouring out what she felt. And she had never meant the HOD to find that out.

ANANYA: So, what shall we do?

KANKANA: I do not wish to punish her. But I also do not support her actions.

Enter Saheb from left.

SAHEB: Ladies, you still have twenty minutes to decide.

ANANYA: This is very hard.

SAHEB: Yes. I am going out to eat. Remember The Gospel According To Saint John.

Exit Saheb from left.

SREETAMA: What did he mean?

ANANYA: I do not know, as I have not read The Bible. I just studied the notes for our Half-yearly exam in the first year.[106]

KANKANA: I bought it. But I do not remember any of the Gospels in particular. All the Gospels tell the life of Jesus, so we just read the first Gospel – according to Saint Matthew.

DEVI: So, if Saheb mentioned the Gospel according to Saint John, he must have said it because there is something in particular, something which is not there in the other Gospels.

SREETAMA: [*To Kankana*] See if you can recall it in twenty minutes. In the meantime, let's eat.

They take out their tiffins and sit on the chairs. Lights fade out.

ACT V

Scene I: Room no. 23.

Enter Indra from left.

INDRA: [*Pointing towards the jury's chairs*] Voices. I need their voices.[107]

Enter Sanjukta from left.

---

[106] It is a convention that a special Half-yearly examination is held for the first years of the English Department, where students answer papers on The Bible, Greek and Roman Mythology.
[107] This is an allusion to *Coriolanus*.

	Sanjukta, I will crush you.
SANJUKTA:	[*Striding to her seat*] My wit will lasso around your two-sided horny strength, and bring you to the ground.
INDRA:	You think too much of yourself.
SANJUKTA:	Don't worry. I cannot usurp your throne in that.
INDRA:	The dignified post I am in now bars me from being ungentle.
SANJUKTA:	An ungentle nature is more prominent amongst gentleness and dignity.
INDRA:	You will not have much to say when I win the case.
SANJUKTA:	Indeed I won't, when you win the case.

Indra is about to say something rude when all students begin to file in. Indra goes back and sits at his place. Sanjukta looks triumphantly at him, then sits. All students take their places as before. Enter the Reporter and the Photographer from left. They take their places. Enter Bishakha from left and looks for Harsh.

Enter Harsh, Maya, Shobha and Panchali, carrying in a wild Ankita.

BISHAKHA: Harsh, I am so sorry I am late.

Harsh goes forward to meet her. The others seat Ankita and stand beside her.

HARSH:	Don't worry. You just missed all the proceedings. [*Aside*] I am thankful that she missed it. [*To Bishakha*] We are all waiting for the jury's decision.

MAYA: Come, come, Harsh. You must take your place.

Harsh and Bishakha sit together.

ANKITA: This is so horrible. I wish none of this had happened.

SANJUKTA: Don't worry. I will pull you out of this.

Enter Saheb from left and sits down on the chair behind the table. He places the camera on the table.

SAHEB: Sara, have you been able to type everything?

SARA: Yes, I have.

Enter Sreetama, Ananya Mukherjee, Devi and Kankana from left. Kankana holds a paper in her hands. They take their seats.

SAHEB: [*To Kankana*] Please read out your decision.

KANKANA: [*Reading*] We, the members of the jury, have reached the unanimous decision that Ankita is… [*Everybody inclines forward. Ankita puts her hands over her face*] not guilty.

There is a loud cheering.

INDRA: [*Rising*] What?

SANJUKTA: [*Rising*] Yes!

SAHEB: I hereby declare Ankita to be acquitted of all charges related to the case of the abusive papers. All possible suspicion on Harsh Chakraborty in relation to this case is hereby dropped due to lack of evidence. The court is dismissed.

He rises. Everyone rises and begins to talk.

BISHAKHA: *You?* Suspected?

HARSH: Dropped, dropped.

BISHAKHA: Related to this case?

HARSH: [*Pleadingly*] Lack of evidence. I am innocent.

BISHAKHA: I heard that. But why *would* you be suspected in the first place?

HARSH: [*Hesitatingly*] It was because of some words that I said.

BISHAKHA: You always make a blunder!

Exit Bishakha from left, Harsh following.

REPORTER: [*Coming up to Saheb*] That was some trial.

SAHEB: Yes, so it was.

PHOTOGRAPHER: [*Coming up*] I need my camera back.

SAHEB: Here. Take it.

He gives it to the photographer.

REPORTER: [*To the photographer*] Well, now let's go out.

Exit Reporter and Photographer from left.

KATHA: Attention please. [*Everyone looks at her*] We have come to the end of the historic trial. This Room no. 23, which has seen history being made, is now proud to have witnessed yet another incident. To everyone who is assembled here, I wish you have all had a lovely time.

Several students rush towards Ankita, who receives them with joyous open hands.

SANJUKTA: I told you I would pull you through.

Exit Indra from left. Other students begin to leave, talking.

KANKANA: Was it about the woman who was about to be stoned, whom Jesus saved, saying, "He who has never sinned, let him cast the first stone"?

SAHEB: Yes.

Barnali comes along.

BARNALI: It was a great trial. I must thank you guys.

KANKANA: Don't mention it.

Exit Saheb from left.

BARNALI: Come, let's go to the canteen.

KANKANA: No, let's go to the Girls' Common Room. Ankita must be there. We must talk to her.

BARNALI: Yes. Let's go. I also want to know what she has to say about it all.

Exit Barnali and Kankana with the other students. Lights fade out.

Scene II: The Lounge.

Pushpita, Sara, Barnali, Ankita, Sanjuktaeogi and Ankit are discovered seated at the lounge.

ANKIT: All's well that ends well.

ANKITA: Well, all was not well for me, but I am glad
                     that it is over, and I am acquitted.

ANUARNA: I do not like to take sides, but you fought off
                     Indra very well.

SANJUKTA: Yes. I am glad I got this chance. Thanks a
                     lot for choosing me, Ankita.

ANKITA: Thanks a lot for taking it for me – and
                     winning the case. I am so glad the jury
                     declared me not guilty.

Enter Saheb from right.

SAHEB: Well, I have submitted your splendidly-
                     typed report of the case to the HOD.

PUSHPITA: What did she say?

SAHEB: She is obviously not happy that no person
                     was found guilty. But she also said that she's
                     glad it's over. She would not like to go
                     through the process again. She is glad that
                     the fuss is over.

ANKIT: What about the fact that she does not know
                     the identity of the composer?

SAHEB: There are many things that one does not
                     know. Even she. So, she'll take it as one of
                     those subjects.

ANKIT: But will she?

SAHEB: I do not speak unless I am sure. If I'm not
                     sure, I say I'm not sure. I am sure she will
                     take it in that way. To quote her, she said,
                     "Well, we cannot know everything, so I
                     guess I will not pursue the matter any more".

PUSHPITA: That's great.

BARNALI: Yeah. That's fantastic. We love her when she's like this.

SAHEB: By the way, that Reporter and that Photographer are in for a surprise.

BARNALI: Well, when I was passing by the corridor after this was all over, I heard the reporter say "It went completely over my head". He said he'd run a report on a particular door of some toilet.

SAHEB: Well, he'll have to do it without pictures, and nobody is going to read that.

SARA: I saw the photographer clicking at a lot of places.

SAHEB: Well, I took the film out of the camera.[108]

ANKIT: That's great! But you shouldn't have done that. It's not yours.

SAHEB: When people use their belongings to do something not right or good, it should be taken away from them.

ANKITA: That's true.

ANKIT: What are you nodding at? You used your pen and paper to write something not *right* – morally, though very true.

---

[108] These were not the days of DSLRs. Only 'point and shoot' cameras were in vogue with the amateurs, but were not used by professionals.

SAHEB:	They were her *feelings*. And she meant no harm.
ANKIT:	But she shouldn't nod.
SAHEB:	Look, the trial is over – the jury has given its written statement. Don't start this all over again.
ANKIT:	I guess you are right. Well, I still feel she shouldn't have nodded.
ANKITA:	I am so sorry.
ANKIT:	That's better. Now, I have to go meet my friends from the Department of Economics.

Exit Ankit from right.

SANJUKTA:	That reminds me, why did you not include an "and" in the poem?

Pushpita and Barnali slap their foreheads; Sara hides a smile.

ANKITA:	[*Disbelievingly*] Are you serious?
SARA:	[*Rising*] Listen you guys. We have to buy some books.
BARNALI:	Don't let *me* keep you.

Exit Sara and Pushpita from right.

SANJUKTA:	Yes, as I was saying – you should have included an "and".
ANKITA:	I thought you just said that to save me at the trial.
SANJUKTA:	[*Rising*] Of course I used it to your advantage. But I am serious. Tell me.

Exit Sanjukta and Ankita from right, talking.

BARNALI: Well, I am the only freak who's normal over here. Wow! That was a beautiful epigram! [*Reflecting*] Hey, I have become *reflexive* towards figures of speech. [*Rising*] Now, I must go to the library for my next assignment. She has not given any yet, but I must prepare myself.

Exit Barnali from right. Lights fade out.

CURTAIN